"What in God's name have you done, Mickey?"

Harry snatched at her hand, pulling it in front of him. "Explain this!" he roared as he jiggled her ring finger.

"It's only an engagement ring, Harry," Mickey responded hesitantly, confused by the lightning flashing from Harry's deep brown eyes.

"I know what it is," Harry grated through clenched teeth. "I want to know why! To whom! And quickly!"

"George Armstead, that's who!" Mickey's temper flared. "He's a fine, trustworthy man, and we're going to be married. A girl *can* get married without permission when she's eighteen in this state, Harry Butterworth. And you don't have a darned thing to say about it. Do you hear me!"

"I hear you," Harry said, suddenly calm. "Yes, yes, of course you can."

Mickey was dazed. This wasn't the Harry she remembered. The Harry she knew would never give in without a fight.

EMMA GOLDRICK describes herself as a grandmother first and an author second. She was born and raised in Puerto Rico, where she met her husband, a career military man from Massachusetts. His postings took them all over the world, which often led to mishaps—such as the Christmas they arrived in Germany before their furniture. Emma uses the places she's been as backgrounds for her books, but just in case she runs short of settings, this prolific author and her husband are always making new travel plans.

Books by Emma Goldrick

HARLEQUIN PRESENTS

HARLEQUIN ROMANCE

Don't miss any of our special offers. Write to us at the following address for information on our newest releases.

Harlequin Reader Service
901 Fuhrmann Blvd., P.O. Box 1397, Buffalo, NY 14240
Canadian address: P.O. Box 603,
Fort Erie, Ont. L2A 5X3

EMMA GOLDRICK

my brother's keeper

Harlequin Books

TORONTO • NEW YORK • LONDON
AMSTERDAM • PARIS • SYDNEY • HAMBURG
STOCKHOLM • ATHENS • TOKYO • MILAN

Harlequin Presents first edition July 1988
ISBN 0-373-11087-1

Original hardcover edition published in 1988
by Mills & Boon Limited

Printed in U.S.A.

CHAPTER ONE

HARRY parked the car quietly and came around the side of
the house, along the deep veranda that marked its front.
The day was hot, but here in the shade of the trees that
sheltered the area a cool breeze plucked at maple leaves,
casting a dappled searchlight across the girl's bright red
hair. The air was redolent of high summer in the
Adirondack Mountain lake country.

He stopped with one foot up on the first step when he
caught sight of her. Michele was lying at the edge of the
grass, just where the land dropped off for about two feet on
to the sandy beach that surrounded the cove. He set his bag
down softly, and moved in her direction as silently as he
could.

She was stretched out haphazardly on her stomach, hands
cupped to support her chin as she stared out over Milisquic
Lake. Her jeans were so worn that their seat was white.
Mickey was wearing a cast-off man's shirt, tied across in
front to leave a band of lightly tanned skin on view. One of
her feet was kicking at the grass as if keeping time with
some music running through her mind.

It was so quiet that one could actually hear the rustle of
the leaves, the brief spurt of wings as robins scoured the
grass, the occasional whisper as a tiny wavelet broke on the
shore. So quiet that when his foot landed on a twig lying in
the grass it snapped loudly. The girl whirled around to a

5

sitting position, startled. The freckles across the bridge of her stubby nose stood out against the pale white of her face. Her grey eyes had trouble focusing as she peered into the shade behind her. But only for a moment.

She came gracefully to her feet. It almost seemed she was running before she actually was fully up. 'Harry!' she yelled in great glee, and threw herself up at him, arms around his neck.

He gathered her in and twirled her round, her feet flying a full six inches off the ground, her nose at his. 'Harry, Harry, Harry!' she whispered in his ear, each sounding like a caress.

They went around in a circle one more time. He was laughing as he set her down. 'What's the matter, Mickey? You act as if you've never seen a man before!'

'Don't talk like that,' she said solemnly as she leaned back, still in the shelter of his arms, and examined his craggy face hungrily. 'What good does it do a girl to have a big brother if he's never around when she needs him?'

He lifted her up again to plant a kiss on the tip of her nose. Her arms went around him eagerly, clutching as if at a great prize. 'Mickey Devlin Butterworth,' he said His husky baritone rolled over her. She buried herself in the sound, hugging all the tighter. When he gently disentangled her, she moaned a little protest.

He pushed her away, far enough to examine the gamine face, the unruly pigtails, the slender form. 'You haven't grown an inch,' he told her.

'I have so,' she squeaked, drawing herself up to her full five foot four, throwing her shoulders back, holding in a deep breath.

'I meant up, not out. Breathe, you crazy kid. You'll turn

blue if you keep that up.'

The air gushed out of her in a great sigh. 'I know what sort of girl *you* like, Harry Butterworth. Only I can't hold my breath long enough!'

He pulled her back against him. She hid her face just under the third button of his shirt, and sniffled.

'How's the old man?'

'Harry, Papa—I mean, your father—isn't well at all. He won't tell me anything, and the doctor won't say a word. But he looks tired all the time.'

'There you go again,' he chuckled. 'I know what you call him when I'm not around, but the minute I show up it's always 'your father'. What's with you?'

Her arms fumbled to reach around him, without a great deal of success. He was not a handsome man, but he was solidly built, and under his thin open-necked shirt was all muscle. 'You know, Harry, when my mother married your father I thought Christmas had come for the second time in one year. I always have this guilty feeling about you and—Papa. As if I were stealing him away from you, or something. Hey, I'd been telling my mother for years we needed a man around the house, and then on my eighth birthday she produced the *two* of you. I think I fell in love with you both, right then.'

He had turned her around so they were walking arm in arm up towards the house. 'Of course, your father was much more handsome, and not at all mean, and not such a big tease——' His arm tightened around her. 'I don't want you to have a swelled head,' she giggled.

'I'm sure I won't,' he returned. 'Not with you hanging behind me, whispering in my ear. Isn't that what all the Roman conquerors had to put up with during their triumphs?'

'How would I know?' she sighed. 'I've never been to Rome. Unless you mean Rome, New York?'

'Oh, cut it out. Poor put-upon Mickey. You've had your chances. And there's no need for you to feel you were stealing my dad. After all, I stole your mother completely.' They were at the stairs now, he still on the ground, she up two stairs, and almost at his height. 'No crying, now,' he adjured. 'Mama straightened *me* out in a hurry. I miss her.'

'Me, too.' The words bore their own witness to sorrow, but it didn't last; five years had softened the blow. They were laughing again as they went up on to the porch.

'He's sleeping,' she cautioned. 'He sleeps every afternoon, for an hour or so. Why don't we sit in the swing until he——Unless you need a drink, and—and everything?'

'I don't need a thing,' he said. 'I stopped in Miller's Gap before coming up to the house.'

She tried to squeeze him affectionately, but there was no give to his frame. He laughed down at her, helping her into the sofa-swing on the deep-shaded porch. She settled down, tucking her feet up under her, grinning up at him as he settled in beside her.

'My favourite brother,' she giggled.

'Not exactly a prize,' he laughed. 'Your only brother!'

'So why did you come, Mr Butterworth? I mean, why now?'

'Wow, is it autumn so soon? *Mr Butterworth?* I can feel the chill right off the North Pole. I came because I swore I heard you call me, Mickey. The breeze carried it right across the border into Massachusetts, and all the way to Boston. Come home, Harry, that's what it said. Didn't you call me?'

He was altogether too close to the truth, and she just

could not admit it. She had never been shy before with Harry, and now it just overwhelmed her. The upset brought a stammer to her voice. He used a knuckle to tilt her chin up. 'Hey, I didn't mean to upset you, Mike.'

'Don't call me that,' she sighed. 'I'm a big girl now. Next month I'll be twenty-one.'

'Why, so you will.' His palm smoothed her cheek, bringing the dimple to life. 'Twenty-one. And you were only eight when we first met.'

'Don't you dare say "how time flies",' she challenged him. She straightened her shoulders, flicking a finger at her disarrayed shirt as if some magic touch might make it look glamorous. 'You were the most obnoxious sixteen-year-old I ever knew. Why did you really come back now, Harry?'

His dark brown eyes, masked by heavy brows, seemed to search her face, as if he were looking for just the right words. And then he grinned at her. 'Well, your most earnest wish had come true, Mickey.' She frowned at him.

'Don't call me that,' she said primly. 'My name is Michele.'

'Don't interrupt, Mickey. I'm home to recover from a broken heart. You always said it would happen, and now it has. Smashed to pieces.'

'The trouble with you is you're a lousy actor,' she snapped. 'Don't try to—is it really true, Harry?' Her anxiety could be measured by the ton. A sort of 'they can't do that to my brother' expression fluttered across her face. 'You're pulling my leg, Harry!'

'Not a bit,' he said solemnly. 'Promised to marry me, she did, and then found a man with more money. Hey!' Her arms were around his neck again, hugging tight.

'You mustn't let it get you down.' She was doing her best

to soothe non-existent tears, but it took her a moment to realise that. 'Darn you, Harry, you're doing it again! When will you stop teasing me?'

'No, don't hit me,' he pleaded through the big grin that split his face. 'Poor romantic Mickey. You'll never learn, will you?'

'If I hadn't missed you so much I *would* hit you,' she promised. 'Is it really true? Tell me who this—this bitch is and I'll scratch out her eyes!'

'And what happened to my perfect little lady?' He was laughing again, a deep rumble that seemed to start somewhere south of his stomach and work its way up through his whole frame. 'My little Michele wouldn't use words like that!'

'Yes, she would,' she stated flatly. 'And worse. Just because I've stayed home all these years to look after your father doesn't mean that I—'

'Doesn't mean what?' Another deep voice from behind her, and a creak as the screen door opened. They sound so much alike, she told herself. Father and son. She whirled round and hopped up.

'Harry's here,' she announced happily. 'Papa, Harry's here!'

'Well, I knew that,' the older man growled. 'Who else would set you off into a flaming argument like that, child? Come over here, son.'

She stepped back out of the way, hands tucked primly behind her back, and watched. Harry moved slowly, as if unsure of his welcome. But the last three steps were hastened as they embraced each other. Gregory had been taller, Mickey told herself. Taller and broader and—more distinguished. But no more. It was Harry who was the bigger now. He stretched two inches or more above his father's bent frame, and looked so solid compared to the older man's gauntness. I've lived with Papa Gregory so long I didn't notice, she told herself fiercely, reprimanding. I didn't notice how his hair has gone sparse, how his shoulders droop, how lined his face. God help me, I didn't notice!

When the old man extended a hand to draw her into the family circle she went with a guilty feeling. Harry sensed it. 'None of that, Mickey,' he ordered. She blushed, and was squeezed from both sides.

'My little sister isn't so little any more,' he told his father.

'I know that. That's why I called you. How are things among the practising attorneys of Boston, son?'

'Well, I had an interesting—'

'Whoa,' she interjected. 'If this going to be a lawyers' reunion I'd better start the supper.'

'Bossy little thing,' Gregory commented.

'You noticed?' His son put an arm around his father's shoulders and they went off into the den. 'For conversation,' Harry called back over his shoulder. 'Legal consultations.'

'I know,' she returned with a giggle. 'But I moved the drinks cabinet into the dining-room.' He gave her that demonic expression—eybrows raised, eyes half-closed, mouth straight and firm. She was still laughing as she stuck out her tongue at him and ducked into the kitchen.

Life seems to be so much better this afternoon, she told herself wryly as she danced twice around the big kitchen. But tuna salad and vegetables won't do, now that Harry's home. She sang a little nonsense song as she pawed through the freezer, rescued a couple of man-sized steaks, and shoved them into the microwave oven to defrost. But why had Harry come at this particular time? There were two versions already on view: his father had sent for him, or he was suffering from jilting. That last seemed almost impossible. Harry wasn't handsome, but what woman could possibly turn him down? He had so much—good lord, my brother is the sexiest male in the world, she thought. Twenty-nine years old, a practising attorney. Six foot one. Thick brown hair that has a tendency to curl at the ends—which annoyed him considerably. A wide face, brown eyes, heavy eyebrows. And practically no earlobes. The sign of the devil's children, Mama used to say. And he certainly has some of the devil in him!

She giggled as she danced around the kitchen, sorting vegetables, peeling carrots, arranging a tossed salad, all with one eye on the clock. Papa Gregory was a diabetic. In addition to his insulin and his exercise, he was required to eat by the clock. Four small meals, regularly spaced. And six o'clock was the witching hour.

With all her preparations made she took one quick look around the kitchen, and then dashed upstairs to her own room. The old denims and the man's shirt were gone in a trice. She stuck her head out the door to check. The rumble of voices still continued from downstairs. She chuckled as she stole down the hall, remembering what a lark it had been to do so when she was fourteen. Stealing down the hall in nothing but briefs and a good conscience, dodging the men in her life.

The bathroom was at the end of the hall. She sidled in, closing the door gently behind her. The shower responded instantly with hot water. Her hair barely fitted inside the shower cap, but she crammed away at it. The briefs fell by the wayside as she climbed into the shower stall, and let the water wash away what was left of her melancholy.

'After all, how important is it that George couldn't come last night?' she asked herself. 'He's the most gorgeous male in the world and I'm glad we're finally engaged. But now Harry's here. If he stays long enough. There's nothing better for a girl's morale than to have a big brother to escort one around! Now all I need is a little scheme.' And wouldn't Harry say something about that! Schemer—that was his favourite accusation. 'When all I ever wanted to do was help,' she told the soap in an injured tone. 'It isn't my fault that my schemes don't always work out the way they ought!'

Even the soap seemed to be on Harry's side. It squirted out of her hands and ricocheted around the stall. With half-blinded eyes she went down on hands and knees to trap it.

There was a need to hurry. Not knowing the time, Mickey forgot about the soap, lifted her face into the spray, and jumped out. A cautious peek around the door-jamb indicated the hall was clear of wandering males. She wrapped the bath towel carelessly around her middle and ran for her room.

A demure high-collared dress was her selection for the evening. A light cotton thing, which treated her curves nicely. 'What curves there are,' she groaned, not for the first time, as she tried by deep breathing, pure magic, or incantation to make something massive out of her tiny breasts.

'They're not all that small,' her friend Helen had said. 'Not impressive, but certainly not disreputable. And if you stood just at the right angle, they'd be impressive.' Mickey was sixteen when she got that advice, and a full year of standing at the right angle had followed, with no noticeable success.

But there was one attribute about which she could boast: her lovely hair, freed from its pigtails, fell half-way down her back in a cascade of brilliant red. She sat down at her dressing-table and began the ritual brushing. One hundred strokes, slow and easy, each stroke highlighting the deep gloss of colour, bringing the lovely softness to its greatest glow. She left it free as she dressed, humming an old folk-tune that she loved as she slipped into clean underclothes. Dear Harry's home! There's no end of profit a girl could make out of that! The dress went over her head and zipped satisfactorily in place. She turned twice in front of the mirror to check.

The loose hair would not do, of course. Princesses might sit in a tower window seat with their hair loose, but if they had to get to the kitchen they would have to do something about it. She sported a wry grin as she braided it all and fastened it up a coronet. It was time to go downstairs. Feeling refreshed she skipped down the hall like a child of ten. The voices in the den were still at it. Father and son had a great deal to say to each other. And why not? Harry had come home to Albany last Christmas—just for two days—and hadn't been seen since.

At exactly ten minutes before the hour she put the steaks on the grill, and hurried the table settings in the dinning-room. The two of them were still at it, their deep voices playing counterpoint from the den. She paused at the open door for a second. Not to eavesdrop. No, indeed! Liar! Her argument with herself almost blocked out the conversation. Almost.

'It's all settled,' Papa said slowly. 'Everything nailed

down. Except for Mickey. I just don't know what to do about Mickey. There'll be plenty of money for her—but she needs more than that.' There was a tinge of sorrow in his normally steady voice.

'You needn't worry about Mickey,' Harry assured him. 'I'll take care of her.' A ruminative silence, and then a chuckle from Gregory.

'Then that takes care of that, son. I do wish I could have seen my grandchildren, Harry. A man at my state and age wants to be assured of continuity.'

'Now don't push, Dad. It will all happen. Rest assured of that. And the second boy will be named Gregory.'

'The second? What about the first?'

'Well, that's—good lord, she's burning the supper! *Mickey!*' There was the noise of chairs scraping, and footsteps coming to the door, but by that time Mickey had fled, just in time to rescue the steaks.

Despite all her plans, dinner was fifteen minutes late. She brought the steaks in on individual plates: one huge steak for Harry, the other split in two parts for herself and Gregory. 'I'm sorry, Papa,' she sighed. 'When I get excited I seem to lose the hang of things.'

'You do fine,' Gregory complimented. 'Only I'm glad you're here. Harry. For the past four weeks I've been fed nothing but rabbit food!'

'Now that's not fair.' Mickey ducked behind Papa's chair so he would not see the flush mounting to her cheeks.

'No, it's not,' Gregory conceded. 'I admit it's all that damn fool doctor's orders. I shouldn't take it out on you. You've been very patient with me, housekeeping for the past five years, when you should have gone off to college, mixed with young people.'

'I couldn't have done that!' she gasped.

'Why not?' Harry looked at her for the first time. Stared at her. 'Why not?'

'Because——' She bit her lip, enforcing silence. This was no time to tell them, *Because I promised Mama I wouldn't, that's why.* And what would they think of that for an excuse, these two big Butterworth men?

'Just because——' Harry laughed. 'How many times have I heard that phrase?'

'Rings a bell?' Gregory asked.

'I made some jelly—the kind you can eat, Papa.' But no little diversion of hers was going to get Harry off the trail, she knew.

'A conniving little schemer, that one,' Harry ploughed on. 'Made my life a misery, she did.'

'I did no such thing!' Her little figure snapped to attention as her shoulders went back and her chin came up. 'No such thing, Harry Butterworth!'

'Huh,' he chuckled. 'Do you remember when I broke my arm, Dad?'

'Oh, vaguely,' Gregory returned grinning. 'Was there some secret about it?'

'You bet. Little Mickey just *had* to have some grapes, and Mr Anselm's vines were just ready. She nagged and squeaked at me until I finally gave in. So we sneaked over there under cover of darkness, and we picked a few grapes. But that wasn't enough, was it, Mickey?'

'I was very young then,' she snapped angrily.

'You certainly were,' Harry continued. 'But no, the grapes from low down on the vine wouldn't do. Only the best of them would suit, and those grew up on top of the arbour, right? And if she doesn't get what she wants she's going to cry! And there I am with a bucket full of the evidence, and the lights have come on in Mr Anselm's house. And she's going to cry if I don't climb the arbour and get the grapes on top. How about that?'

'A short and sordid career for an amateur burglar,' his father chuckled. 'So, I take it you climbed?'

'What else could I do? I climbed. And when I get up on the top my foot slipped, and my partner here let out a screech, and I was so startled I fell off the darned thing, and broke my arm.'

'Quite a story. I heard part of it at the time.'

'But it's not over yet, Dad. Look, there I was, lying on the ground with a broken arm, trying to remember what day it was, and there next to me is little Miss Lovely, crying her eyes out. Mr Anselm comes down from the house, growls at me for scaring the poor little girl and—honestly—she can only be comforted by him picking her a bunch of grapes from the top of the arbour!'

'Well, I felt very bad.' Mickey managed to squeeze in an indignant word or two. 'It was a terrible experience, and you were trying to be so brave—because boys never cry, do they?—so I had to. Can't you see that?' she glared at him across the table. 'Mr Anselm was very nice.'

'Yes, he sure was. Butter wouldn't melt in her mouth, let me tell you. And that's the way it went for years and years. I got all the blame; poor Mickey was put upon and must be humoured.'

'A lot you know,' she sniffled, using her napkin to cover her confused expression.

'Ah, there's more?' Those legal eyes of Judge Butterworth bore into her, pulling out truths as if he were practising painless dentistry.

'Yes, there's more,' she sighed. 'I ran on ahead with my grapes, and told Mama. When Harry got there she insisted on bundling him into the car and taking him to the hospital. She wouldn't let me even go with her. It was a big adventure, and she made me go straight to my room and stay there.' The indignation of a ten-year-old flooded her voice. The scene was still vivid in her memory.

'And then——' Her voice was very small, very subdued. 'When she came back home you had squealed on me, Harry Butterworth. I never thought you would do that! For the first time in all my life my mother spanked me!'

Both men stared at her, totally surprised. 'I don't believe it,' Gregory said finally. 'Emily never lifted a hand to anyone, man, woman, or child.'

'Well, she lifted one to me,' Mickey said stubbornly. 'Several times. I couldn't sit down for three days. And it was all your fault, Harry.'

'Yes, I can see that.' He spoke solemnly, but there was laughter in those deep brown eyes. For just a moment she hated him.

Mickey scraped her chair back and snatched at the nearest empty dishes. Her feet moved automatically, carrying her across the hall and through the swinging doors into the kitchen. She was standing at the sink, her back turned, when he came in behind her.

'Hey, you never used to be so prickly,' he said, slipping one arm around her shoulder to comfort. She shrugged it off, moving sideways to escape.

'I'm not prickly.' she snapped at him. 'I'm just—just angry. Now please go away and leave the little girl to do what she does best.'

'Kissing is what I remember,' he joked.

'Dishwashing is what I remember,' she snarled. 'While you lived it up, I was the drudge. Mama never asked *you* to come in the kitchen, did she?' She tilted up her chin and glared at him.

'I can't say that she did,' he admitted calmly.

'Well, that's the way I remember it,' she snapped. 'Michele, do the dishes. Michele, don't make so much noise, the men are working. Huh! I wished many a time I was a boy!'

'What a waste that would have been.' He was ominously close to her. She shuddered, not knowing what was to come. What she got was not at all what she expected.

'How about that jelly you promised?'

'Men,' she grumbled. 'Always thinking of your stomachs!'

'I wasn't thinking of mine so much as Dad's,' he laughed.

'Oh, my! I—I forgot.' She bustled contritely to the refrigerator and took out one glass of decorated jelly.

'Only one?' he asked plaintively.

'Only one,' she sighed. 'No, I'm not picking on you—it's just I didn't know you were coming. You could have a dish of ice-cream—and I made some chocolate chip cookies this morning.'

'I'll take it.' He relieved her of the jelly, and watched as she dived back into the refrigerator for the ice-cream. And he was still too close, she told herself. Close enough to pick the pins out of her hair, and let it fall in one loose braid down her back.

'I—don't do that,' she said warily. Her experience had been limited to local gropers, but he was her brother, for goodness' sake. She stepped away, and concentrated on filling the saucer with ice-cream. When he had both hands filled she felt a strange sense of relief, following him back to the table moments later with the coffee pot and three cups.

'That's what I need,' Gregory announced, reaching for the hot coffee.

'Only one cup,' she reminded him. 'It's decaffeinated, but you still only get one cup. And we have to check your blood sugar before you go to bed tonight.'

The conversation shifted with the coffee. They were back in legal-land, and she was far behind. Knowing they would hardly miss her, she got up again, cleared the table, and washed the rest of the dishes. They were still at it twenty minutes later.

It was a routine she had become accustomed to through the years. The men lingering over the dinner-table for tobacco and talk, the women fading into the kitchen to finish the day's work. But there was no tobacco tonight, she noticed as she tiptoed by the dining-room door.

It was late June in the mountains, but for all that there was a chilly breeze. She picked up a shawl at the door, and went out on to the porch. The swing creaked at her seductively. She walked over and settled herself, leaning back against the metal headboard, tucking her feet up as she always did. The moon was bright over Mount Bernhardt, making a path of light across the still waters of the lake. A loon ruffled the silence. Across the cove, about a mile away, she could see the lights of Miller's Gap, the tiny village that was the centre of life in the area.

In 1890 this part of New York had still been a sylvan wilderness. But then the millionaires had come, building huge sprawling homes with wide rooms, broad verandas and all the comforts of Victorian life. The little village had grown up around them as a holiday resort: a single street with the necessary businesses, and a rackety old wooden pavilion that sprawled along the waterfront, the focus of society life. There was a dance on at the Pavilion, and she had meant to go, but Harry had washed that all out of her mind. And now, cuddling herself into the corner of the swing, she could hear the music drifting in bursts across the lake. The lights were all on over there, too, but not so brightly that they obscured the sky. Orion stood just overhead; the Big Dipper hung low in the northern sky, pointing an accusing finger at Polaris. Mickey took a deep breath, filling her lungs with the sweet scent of pine, with the caress of primrose and columbine.

'So this is where you've got to.' A rhetorical question. She nodded, and swung her feet down to make room beside her. He walked over, casting a huge shadow against the wall as the moonbeams outlined him. She patted the cushions beside her in invitation.

The swing groaned as it accepted his weight. It started a chain of thought. 'How much do you weigh, Harry?'

'Oh, about a hundred and eighty—something like that.'

'Do you still do all that work-out stuff? Handball?'

'Racketball these days,' he chuckled. 'Want to feel my muscles?'

'Don't be silly,' she sighed. 'I've outgrown all those things. Tell me about the girl in Boston.'

'The girl in—oh, that one.' The silence stretched into infinity.

'Harry?' she prompted.

'What?'

'You disappeared there for a while. About the girl in Boston?'

'Ah. Little Miss Nosy? Or sisterly concern?' He shifted

his weight, crossing his right leg over his left knee. The swing was old and tired. It slid him down in her direction, until his thigh was touching hers. She patted him on the knee.

'A little of both, I suppose,' she admitted wryly. 'Tell me.'

'Well, she's very tall, and very well—er—constructed.'

'I know about the birds and the bees,' she teased.

'Yes. She's a blonde—golden blonde, I guess. Nice teeth, lovely legs——'

'You sound as if she were a mare you were appraising, Harry. What *kind* of a girl is she?'

'That's hard for me to describe,' he sighed, 'especially to someone like you, Mickey. She's—high society—I guess that's the best I can think of. She likes parties, and opera, and "good works". She wants to live a rich life, she wants a yacht and European travel, and she changed her mind about marrying me. How's that?'

'I think that's cruel. Did you love her very much?'

'Not much, I suspect,' he chuckled. 'It was just that the marriage thing was going around, and I suppose I caught the germ. So I courted her for six months, popped the question, and she accepted. And then I went home and thought. A month later she changed her mind.'

Mickey leaned closer to him, resting one hand on his shoulder. Her long thin pianist's fingers dug into his shirt in sympathy. 'And what did you conclude?' she asked softly.

'I concluded that I'd been a damned fool,' he said, laughing from deep in his throat. 'I concluded I already had the whole world in my hand, and I had no real use for a society woman from Beantown.'

Her hand made patting motions on his shoulder. One of

his big hands came up and trapped hers, warming it with affection. 'I was wrong, Mickey,' he said softly. 'You're all grown up. In every way.'

'I—could you stay for the summer?' she stammered.

'I intend to. Why?'

'Well, there are a lot of girls who come,' she murmured. 'I could arrange for you to meet them, and I could——'

'Whoa up,' he laughed, stretching up to his feet. 'The last thing in the world I want is for you to dream up one of your grade A schemes, Mike. I think I can meet all the girls I want to without your help. It would be a wonderful summer if you would kindly refrain from do-gooding, Miss Michele Devlin Butterworth,'

'Why, that's mean,' she muttered. 'You need help. I'll bet if I had been in Boston we could have brought your blonde lady to heel as easy as pie! You really need me, Harry!'

'Like I need a hole in my head,' he laughed. 'I'm going for a walk. Want to come?'

'I can't,' she sighed. 'It's time for Papa's blood test.'

'He can't do that himself?'

'Well, he can do it all,' she said, 'except for the first step. You have to get a drop of blood to put on the test-strip. Papa's a wonderful man, but he just doesn't have the courage to take the little needle and stick it in his own finger.'

'Oh, wow!' Harry laughed, and then turned serious. 'Don't you ever imagine for a minute, Mickey, that I don't appreciate how much loving care my father gets from you. You've sacrificed a great deal, and you've made him very happy.'

He was standing on the top step of the veranda, extending a hand in her direction. She flowed gracefully up from the swing and accepted the hand. He's still taller than I am, she told herself in surprise. He's standing a step lower than me, and I still have to look up at——

The thought was blotted from her mind as his head came down to her, lips touching gently. Not in all her years had she ever kissed her brother in just this way. She sagged against the roof post as he let her go, turned, and walked briskly down towards the water. She watched him all the way, until he turned left, away from the route to Miller's Gap, and disappeared behind the trees that blocked her view.

'Mickey?' Papa Gregory was calling from inside. She shrugged her shoulders, searched for her shawl, and went back in. He had assembled all the material for the test: the alcohol swab, the tube of test-strips, the cotton wool, the battery-operated machine that did the actual counting. And the short blue needle, with less than an eighth of a centimetre of sterilised steel showing, that actually made the puncture.

'I thought I would do it myself,' Papa Gregory said, 'but I still don't have the nerve. What are you thinking about?'

She dropped her shawl over the nearest chair and concentrated on the work before her. The alcohol swab made her hand cool. She scrubbed Papa Gregory's index finger, pulled the cap off the needle, and unconsciously bit at the end of her tongue. 'Are you ready?'

'I'm never going to be ready. What were you thinking?'

'Well, I was talking to Harry, and he needs my help.'

'So?'

'But as usual, he doesn't know that yet. I'm going to help him anyway.' With that last word she drove the needle down into Gregory's finger, and he yelled.

'Did that hurt?' she asked anxiously, hurrying to get the bleeding finger on to the test-strip.

'Not at all,' he chuckled. 'You're a dangerous young lady. I hope that Harry appreciates all the help he's going to get.'

'Well, he won't,' she said sadly. 'Years and years from now he'll think about it, and maybe then he'll thank me. But I'm going to help him anyway. Don't wiggle like that, you'll smear the sample.'

She went up to bed just after the blood test, not because she was tired, but because she had to think. Schemes just didn't pop to mind; they had to be carefully considered. The thinking took a great deal of the night, with her sitting on her window-seat, watching the path of the moon.

Harry came back to the house at eleven o'clock, moving softly for such a big man. She heard him let himself into the kitchen and exchange a few words with his father. His footsteps sounded hollowly on the uncarpeted stairs. A few minutes later she heard the pipes gurgle as he took a shower.

'I *will* help him, whether he likes it or not,' she muttered fiercely. 'He needs a wife, and I'm going to find him one. I mean, I'm going to help him find one.'

She tumbled into bed, so tired that her muscles complained, so tense that she could not drop off. She struggled and twisted, unable to find comfort, and then, in the hazy time between awake and asleep the dream came. It was not a new dream, this. She had first dreamed it when she was fourteen. Every year since then it had appeared as it willed, growing longer, more detailed, each time. She had tried once to explain it to her mother, but had been too embarrassed to get the words out. When she was old enough to make sense of it, her mother was long dead.

So it came to her tonight, slipping into her room through the windblown curtains. First, just a presence, as if a voice had spoken in her ear. 'I'm here, Mickey,' it seemed to say. The voice made her body tingle. She lay still, arms and legs sprawled out casually. Then the presence came to the bed. The mattress sagged beside her, and a wisp of something stripped off the straps of her nightgown, leaving her naked in the middle of the bed, squirming.

The hands again, tantalising. Running slowly down from her cheek, down across the hollow of her throat, lingering on the upper curves of her breasts. She seemed to be paralysed, unable to do anything of her own volition. Ghost-fingers ran up the bronzed tip of her breast, stiffening it suddenly with a rare desire she had not known could be. Another hand wandered down across her slightly rounded belly, into the depths of her, trailing fire and panic after it.

The weight, next. The weight of *him*, coming down on her, squeezing between her legs, agitating against her pelvic bones in a slow grinding motion that drove her senses wild. She could actually feel the warm touch of his lips, on each cheek, on her lips, trailing down the same path the errant ghostly hand had taken, until he was tasting her roseate nub, nibbling on it, drawing her into himself while she moaned and rocked her hips, and begged for—what, she did not know.

Then, in the dream sequence, her hands went free. She ran her fingers through the mat of his hair as he nursed at her breast. Unable to restrain herself, her hands seized on his head and forced it up, and she looked. He had no face!

In that instant, always, the dream disappeared, bringing her back to total awareness, writhing and squirming and moaning with the frustration of it all, her eyes darting across the room to find him. But he was never there. Only the wind, blowing the curtains out.

Wearily, knowing she would never sleep now if she did not, she pulled herself out of the bed, found her old running-suit in the dark, and made her way quietly out of the house. A mile, five miles, whatever. Sooner or later her driving muscles would exorcise the memory, and leave her free to sleep.

Up the hill, pounding, careful of the dark footing. Who could he be? In her earliest crude representations, she had put a face to the dream—a sturdy young football player at her high school. One brief experience in the back seat of his old car had shown her—almost too late—that he was not the one.

Down the other side of the slope, haring home now, the porch lights guiding her. When George had first come courting, three months earlier, she had, on one wild night, concluded that his was the face. It was one of the reasons why she had agreed to marry him. And that's obviously true, she told herself as she pounded up the strip of lawn between the house and the water. It *has* to be George. We'd better get married quickly. I'll die if I have to repeat this crazy dream and never know the ending!

Across the lake the moon laughed.

CHAPTER TWO

NO PRACTISED schemer goes charging into things, and Mickey was more than practised. Her brother would certainly not bite at any casual offering. No thinking fish—er, man—would. So the thing to do was select some interesting bait, and wait to see what happened. With that happy thought in mind, she dressed early: a simple sundress that treated her humble body with elegance; hair brushed to gleaming red, tied back into a ponytail. With a ribbon, no less, rather than her usual shoelace. 'Serious business requires formality,' She giggled at herself in the mirror. She was as light as laughter, coming downstairs at six-thirty to make breakfast.

Bacon and scrambled eggs, prepared and set aside on a warming tray. Hot, strong black coffee. The Butterworth men used it as a morning transfusion. Bread in the toaster, waiting for their arrival before being pushed down into the maw of the machine. Enough? A few pork sausages, just in case. And then the usual orange juice. The bacon and sausages had to be specially selected, to be sure they contained no sugar. As did everything else she bought. It made shopping slow, for every wrapper had to be read for ingredients, and then presented to Papa in delightfully decorated but carefully measured quantities. All that, plus his insulin and carefully controlled exercise, let him live a full life.

She was standing in front of the gas cooker, browning the

sausages, when she heard movement behind her, and a pair of strong arms came around her waist and offered a gentle hug. 'I'm hungry.' Harry's lips were just at her ear, sending a little tingle up and down her spine. She leaned back into him for a moment, offering a sort of armless hug, and then went back to her work.

'It'll be on the table in five minutes,' she said, squirming to get away from the finger that tickled her just below her ribcage. 'Don't *do* that, Harry. Do you want to spoil the breakfast?'

'Rather the breakfast than the cook,' he chuckled. 'I believe that good-looking girls should be cuddled before the eggs are.'

'Stop it, Harry, for goodness' sake. I'm not good-looking, the eggs are coddled, not cuddled, and I'm your sister, not your girlfriend.'

He turned her around to face him, removing the spatula that she waved aimlessly in front of him . 'Two out of three aren't bad,' he laughed. 'You *are* beautiful, and you're my stepsister. I don't know about that other. I never coddled an egg.'

The laughter disappeared from her face. She had the curious feeling that an earthquake was stirring the floor beneath her feet, and yet nothing else was moving. 'But I *am* your sister,' she said cautiously.

'How about that,' he sighed, reaching for a sausage. 'There's a world of difference. Damn, I burned the end of my finger!'

'Well you shouldn't be trying to pick sausages up off the griddle with your bare hands,' she lectured. 'Which one?'

He offered his index finger for inspection. 'We're all out of burn balm,' she said. 'I—oh, I know.' She took his finger gently, and led it up to her mouth.

'Well, that's unusual,' he chuckled. 'Mama kisses it and makes it better?'

'A lot you know,' she returned. 'That's just what Mama used to do. And it works. Doesn't it?'

'Darned if you aren't right. I'm convinced. Now what?'

'Now you take some of that unsalted butter in the refrigerator—not that—up on the top shelf. The white butter. And smear a little of it over the burn. And then you repeat after me——'

He came back from the refrigerator with that broad grin on his face. 'Repeat what?'

'Repeat—that was a stupid thing to do and I will never do it again.'

'I swear,' he chuckled. 'I'm too hungry to do the rest right now. Can we eat?'

'Sit down at the table. No, not that one. That's Papa's chair.'

'And you serve the table every day?'

'Of course I do.' Mickey stopped uncertainly, in the middle of following her well-worn path between stove and table. 'That's my job, you know. I keep house for Papa.'

'Lucky Papa.'

'Oh, you darned tease. Eat your breakfast, Harry. I hope it chokes you. No, I don't, either. I don't care what you think; you're the only brother I have and I love you!'

She stood over him, watching as he ate. He went about the whole affair in leisurely fashion, giving every morsel his undivided attention. When the plate was clean he wiped his lips with a napkin, and gave a huge sigh of contentment.

'You don't eat with the menfolk?'

'Of course I do. Did you think I was some Victorian miss?'

'The house is,' he said, 'I'm not sure about the miss.'

'For your information, I wait until Papa comes down,' she said huffily, and turned away from him. That feeling of uneasiness continued to haunt her. *My stepsister.* He had never ever used that term to her before. There was a difference that hurt. She sniffed to force back a tear, and went moodily to the window. The lake was ruffled today. A gusty wind was kicking up miniature white-caps. A couple in the distance were having trouble managing their canoe.

'Good coffee,' he said. The words came to her as from a distance, hollow, vibrating. She could hear the noises as he shoved back his chair and came across the room behind her. 'I didn't mean to upset you, Mike. Come on now.'

'I'm not upset,' she snapped, whirling around at him with a single tear standing out on her cheek.

'Not much,' he said mournfully. 'If you were any more upset I'd run for the cyclone cellar. How far do I have to humble myself to get back in your good book?'

It was just the opening she needed. The scheme was about to unroll. 'A long way,' she said primly. 'You have to come shopping with me. We're out of lots of things.'

'Shopping?' He had all the caution of a confirmed bachelor. 'As far as Gloversville?'

'No, silly. Right here in Miller's Gap. It's groceries we need, not pretties.'

'I wouldn't be much use,' he chuckled, relieved. 'I don't know a thing about groceries.'

'I'm not renting your mind,' she admonished. 'Groceries come heavy. I'm renting your muscles. Right after I see to Papa.'

'How about that?' he jeered as his father came into the kitchen. 'Here I spent years getting a degree in law, and all she wants is my muscles.'

'Deservedly so,' Gregory chuckled. 'I could hear you two arguing all the way up in my room. But then you always did, didn't you? Argue, that is. It makes things seem like old times.'

'Breakfast is ready, Papa.' She hurriedly fixed his plate and carried it to the table. 'And because your sugar count was so low last night, I thought you could have a sausage.'

'Glorious,' Gregory chuckled. 'A whole one all for myself?' He looked over his shoulder at his son. 'There are times when she has the nerve to cut one in half for me. And you notice nothing else gets put on the table. What I get to eat is on my plate, and she doesn't know the meaning of the word "seconds".'

'Papa!' she said, exasperated. 'You know what the doctor said.'

'I know,' Gregory sighed. 'But you must see, love, that his original directions no longer apply. He wanted me to have a long, happy life . . . But that's enough of that. You two have plans?'

I was thinking of going fishing,' Harry answered, 'but somehow I seem to have been trapped into a shopping expedition.'

'You're behind the times, son. The lake is dead. There hasn't been a fish to be had in the past year. Acid rain, they tell me. Besides, your sister needs a little encouragement. That wimp she's——'

'Papa!'

'OK, OK. I surrender. I won't bring the subject up again.'

'If you do,' she said grimly, 'there'll be ground glass in your supper.'

'Maybe that will improve its taste,' Harry teased, and then ducked as she swung a right hook in his general direction.

'None of that,' his father chided. 'Our Mickey has become an outstanding cook and bottle-washer. The girl has a brain, son.'

'But sometimes she keeps it in her bag,' Harry returned.

'Oh you—you——' She sputtered in the face of the joint laughter. It was always that way. Her temper outraced any logical thinking when her brother was on the tease. Chagrined, she stomped out of the kitchen and went upstairs to her room.

It took five minutes to settle herself down; five minutes in which to think. Something strange had happened in that familiar kitchen this morning, and she was not sure what it was. Something different with Harry. He was still the same solicitous, loving tease—but something more as well. And I have to go into town today, she thought.

Wearily, she got up and went over to her bureau. Hidden away in the second drawer, behind all the soft silky lace briefs that she enjoyed, was a tiny jewellery box. Her hands siezed on it and brought it out, almost reluctantly. And that's another thing, she told herself fiercely. Why so reluctant these past two weeks or more? George is certainly the best catch in my world; but that world is fairly well constricted, and George Armstead is one of the few men of marriageable age who lived within it.

Her engagement ring was a pale gold circle furtively sporting the tiniest of diamonds. Until this moment its size had not bothered her. After all, George had not yet established himself. He had lost the hunting camp his father had left to him, given up as a painter, and his novel had not yet quite caught on. 'But it will,' she muttered to herself. 'After all, I've only faith to give him.' She brushed aside the fact that faith was not the only thing he wanted these days. After all, they were both young, nubile. These sorts of problems were bound to arise in a long engagement. 'Until you're twenty-one,' George kept saying, more like a threat than a promise. Poor dear George. She slipped his ring on her finger. That was another thing George could not understand—why she would only wear his ring outside her home. No matter how many times she had explained about Papa, and not wanting to upset him, George just could not see it.

'Hey, are you coming?' Harry, bellowing from the foot of the stairs. No indeed, nothing had changed. Mickey practised a smile or two, snatched up her bag and cheque book, and bustled along.

'Still mad at me?' He held the car door open for her. His own car. A Mercury Monarch, no less. She sank into the cushions with a sigh of contentment.

'No, I'm not mad at you, silly. What a wonderful car. Lawyering must pay very well. Do you represent a Mafia Don or something?'

'No such luck,' he chuckled. 'I wade through thousands of sheets of corporate papers, and make wise statements about income taxes, interest-bearing bonds, and things like that.'

'It sounds incredibly boring,' she giggled. Her hair was coming loose. She lifted her left hand to brush it back in place, just as he turned to admire it.

'Your hair is always—what the hell——?'

He snatched at her hand, pulling it over in front of him. 'What in God's name have you done?' Inside the closed car his roar was equal to the bellow of a gored bull.

'Please,' she managed to squeak. 'You're squeezing my fingers off!'

'And you damned well deserve it,' he muttered. 'This thing. Explain!' He jiggled her ring finger back at her.

'Harry, that hurts!' She bit at her lip to hold back the tears. And the words. It had never crossed her mind that getting engaged was such a big thing. First Papa Gregory had frowned and made some mumbling remark about 'not until you're twenty-one, girl'. And here her loving brother was treating her as if leprosy spots had appeared between her fingers.

He threw her hand back at her, and guided the car over to the side of the road. 'Now. Explain!'

There was thunder rumbling in his voice, and lightning flashing from those deep brown eyes. 'I don't have to,' she tried tentatively.

'You'd better, or I'll break your bloody neck!' he roared. Her spirit of independence promptly took flight. He would. He was that sort of man.

'It's only an engagement ring.' That explanation floated out on suspicious air, and fell flat on the ground at her feet. The glare was still in his eyes, and the thunder was getting worse.

'I know *what* it is,' he roared. 'I want to know why! And who! And quickly!'

'Well—I—that is, we——'

'We who?'

'George and I. George Armstead. He used to come up every summer. His father was a merchant banker in the city. Don't you remember?'

'My God! That one! An obnoxious kid. He's a two-time

loser. What the blazes is he doing sniffing around you? Is it the money?'

'That's a terrible thing to say to me,' she blustered. 'He——We're in love. And I don't have any money. You know that.'

'Yeah, I know that, but does he? Or does he just look at that great big house, and the fancy cars, and how sick Dad is——'

'That's terrible! Don't you say that!' Her temper was out of hand, could not be recalled. 'Just don't you talk about the man I love, Harry Butterworth. He's a fine, trustworthy man, and we're going to be married.'

'When?'

'I—don't really know. Right after my birthday, I suppose. Although we needn't. A girl can marry without permission when she's eighteen in New York State. And you don't have a darned thing to say about it. Not—a—thing! Do you hear me, Mr Butterworth!'

'I hear you,' he grumbled. 'And I suppose everyone between here and Montreal can, too. God, what a mess. No wonder Papa——' As she watched his face she could almost see him change his mind, move to another path.

'Yes, of course,' he agreed calmly. 'A girl your age is certainly able to marry where she chooses.' He started the motor again, and moved back out on to the road, leaving her more upset than if he had yelled and yelled. She glued her eyes on the dirt road that wound around the knee of Mount Bernhardt and finally joined up with Route 309, the paved road that served as the main street of Miller's Gap.

Just outside the town she tapped him on the shoulder. He slowed down and looked in her direction. 'What did you mean,' she asked anxiously, 'when you said George was a two-time loser?'

'Mean? Did I have to mean anything?'

'Harry, stop teasing. It's important.'

'Of course it is, love. I only meant that he's been married before. Not too successfully, I've heard. But don't take it to heart. I've been away a long time, and I may have heard the wrong gossip. Right?'

'Yes. That's probably true,' she said, in a very unbelieving voice. 'I want to go to the supermarket. Why don't you park by the Pavilion and we can walk over?'

'There's some reason we can't drive right to the door?'

'Oh, Harry, you've become strictly a town-bird. Look, it's a beautiful June day, the sun is bright, the wind is cool, and we're not in a hurry. Why not walk?'

He flashed her a grin—the sort that wore away all her worries—and swung the Mercury off the road into the gravelled parking area. 'The old place hasn't changed a bit,' he commented, looking up at the massive gingerbread construction.

'It has, too,' Mickey giggled. 'They painted the cupola last year.'

'Nobody wants a smarty,' he threatened. She ducked out of the car, unable to entirely escape his swing at her plump posterior.

'That hurt,' she complained, rubbing the affected part.

'Let it be a lesson,' he returned in his best courtroom voice. She laughed and took his arm, cuddling close to him as they walked up the street. This is it, she told herself laughingly. Step number one. Michele Butterworth strolls up the street arm in arm with her big young rich brother. Somebody's bound to notice. Somebody did, but it wasn't quite the notice that she wanted.

'Hey, Michele!' She looked over her shoulder, startled. George Armstead was on the veranda of the Friendly Ice Cream store with his cousin Veronica. Not that George was a problem. But his cousin—oh, lord, that was different. Veronica was on the verge of thirty, with a peculiar kind of beauty. No single part of her—face, hair, figure, eyes, brain—was worth a look. But put them all together and she became a latter day Mata Hari.

What I need, Mickey told herself, is some plump little clinging darling who will give Harry a taste of womanhood, but not be too sweet for his digestion. And this, Veronica isn't!

There's a difficulty in living in villages, as in Miller's Gap, where there was only one street, and where, at that moment, there were only four people in sight; it became impossible to ignore a hail. Discouraged, she tugged Harry to a stop. 'There's somebody you just have to meet,' she sighed.

'Have to? I thought we were just going to buy some groceries? I still want to drop a fishing-line in the lake. All that stuff about there being no fish at all sometimes can mean there are no competent fishermen in the neighbourhood. Have I met these people before?'

If he hadn't, he was about to. The Armsteads came down off the veranda into the dirt path that masqueraded as a pavement, and headed straight for them. 'You knew him years ago,' she muttered. 'Smile.'

'I'm smiling. They'd better hurry. This is only a five-minute smile. After that you have to put a coin in my meter.'

'Don't overdo your part,' she muttered, and then turned to the other couple. 'George, Veronica.' She took two

hesitant steps forward and kissed George on the cheek. He
had never been one for public demonstrations between
them, but he did offer a little hug. 'How nice to see you. Do
you remember my brother, Harry?'

'I can't say that I do,' the tall, blonde woman said. 'And
I'm sure I'd never forget if I had.' Sickening, Mickey
thought. A grown woman drooling in the middle of the
street. Veronica moved in on Harry like a laser bomb
heading for its target. Somehow, in the jostling, Mickey lost
her place at her brother's side and found herself displaced,
and miffed.

Harry quickly demonstrated he had learned a thing or
two about sophistication during his years in Boston. He
offered Veronica a huge smile, squeezed her hand, and
gently set her aside. 'My sister and I haven't seen each other
for some time,' he explained, taking Mickey's elbow. 'And
is this you—fiancé?'

'Yes,' Mickey said hesitantly. All of a sudden the word
'fiancé' had a curious ring to it. 'George,' she added. 'You
remember George? We all played together?'

'Did we really?' He extended a hand and made the
briefest of contacts. George evidently found no pleasure in
it, for he winced, and then seemed considerably relieved to
have his hand back. 'And this is the man you're going to
marry?'

'Of course,' George answered gruffly. 'When Michele is
twenty-one.'

'Let us hope you can make her happy,' Harry said
sombrely. Mickey snatched a quick look up at his face. His
expression was as smooth as whipped cream, but deep in his
eyes was a gleam that seemed to carry a message of its own.

'I'm sure we'll be happy,' she hurriedly interjected. 'I'm

sure——' Her babbling faded in the face of that stern face. I don't remember Harry like this at all, she thought. Never like this!

'Mickey is someone precious to us Butterworths,' Harry went on as if nobody had said a word. 'If I were to find somebody who made her unhappy I'd tear his guts out.' All said in a quiet, almost soft voice that made the threat entirely believable. At least George seemed to think so. He took one or two steps away from them, and fiddled with his tie before working up the courage to say something.

'I think I can make Michele happy,' he said. At each word his courage grew. By the end of the sentence he was his old aggressive self. Michey felt a chill, as if a cold stray wind had isolated her out of all the crowd to blow upon.

'Of course he can,' she added. And then, without thinking, 'I expected you at the house last night, George. What happened?'

'I—er—something unexpected came up. Business, you know.' He drew himself up to his full height, almost an inch taller than Harry, but not at all muscular, as Harry was. His long blond hair brushed the collar of his shirt. He breathed confidence, but a thin bead of perspiration stood out on his too-handsome forehead. 'I dabble in real estate now, Butterworth. Lots of profit in real estate.'

'I'm glad to hear that,' Harry said curtly. 'Mickey is accustomed to the best. You'll need a bundle of money to keep her.'

George was not quite smooth enough to suppress the look of surprise that flashed across his face. Veronica gazed thoughtfully at them both. 'Well, we have to be moving along,' Harry added. 'I don't have a great deal of time to invest in shopping, and that's what we're up to. Perhaps we can get together some other time, Armstead. I'd like to tell you about some of the criminal cases I've prosecuted.' With which he tucked Mickey's arm under his own, and practically dragged her up the street toward the market.

'Harry Butterworth,' she gasped, digging in her heels. 'What the devil do you think you're doing, telling all those lies?' She looked over her shoulder to where the Armstead cousins were deep in some violent argument. 'They—you—criminal cases, huh! You're a corporation lawyer. You told me so yourself!'

'So I lied,' he chuckled. 'The first law of the adult jungle, love, is to be sceptical.'

'You don't have to teach me,' she grumbled. 'I'm sceptical enough for two people. That's what comes of growing up with you for a brother.' She turned around and called back to the other couple.

'George, you won't forget that we're going blueberrying tomorrow? I'll bring the lunch!' Her fiancé gave her a casual wave of his hand and turned back to his argument.

Harry had his hand on her again. Not a gentle grip, that. She squeaked a protest, but went along with him willy-nilly. 'Is that as fast as you can walk?'

'Yes, it is,' she snapped. 'Which one was the lie?'

'I plead the Fifth Amendment,' he returned. 'I am not required to make any statement that might incriminate me.'

'Lawyer talk,' she sputtered. 'Just what are you up to?'

'Testing,' he chuckled. 'Just testing. Not a very romantic meeting, huh? No passionate exchanges?'

'In the public street?' she gasped. 'What do you think I am? An exhibitionist? And then, a little sadly, 'George doesn't care for public displays. He prefers we keep our engagement to ourselves.'

'I can see I'm sadly miseducated,' he said mournfully. 'That's what comes of concentrating on law instead of wine and women.'

'No song? Wine, women and song?'

He pulled her to a stop and squared around, facing her. 'And that's another thing.' He made it sound like a grievous sin. 'I've been home for half a day, and you haven't played anything at all for me. I suppose passion has replaced piano in your young life?'

'No such thing, Harry,' she stammered. 'I—practise every day!'

'I'm glad to hear that.' He was down off his mystery pose, to become the young man she had always loved. 'You are all the song I ever needed, Mike. Don't you forget that.'

They were walking down the second aisle of the tiny market before she came to her senses, having bought ten items, six of which were not suitable.

'Close your mouth, Mike,' he said, reaching over a big finger to do that for her. She gulped, shook herself, and settled down to the real business of life.

In the end they accumulated so many bags of groceries that Harry pushed the shopping trolley out to the pavement, and gave her orders to wait while he went for the car. And just to make sure she obeyed, he put both hands on her shoulders and kissed her gently on the forehead. He might not have meant it to be so, but Mickey fell back into her daze again, and her feet stuck in place as if they were glued there.

It was the unexpected that brought her back to reality. 'Michele!' A high-pitched squeal of delight, right in her ear, snapped her around. And there's the answer to a maiden's prayer, Mickey told herself, laughing.

'Sue Ellen! I didn't know you had come. Are you here for the summer?'

The plump little brunette was even shorter than herself, but skilfully designed to encompass a great deal of woman in a small package. But Sue Ellen Swanson was the sort of girl who didn't seem to know all that. Exactly what I need for Harry, Mickey assured herself. The perfect lawyer's wife!

'Yes, we're here for the whole summer,' Sue Ellen averred. 'Mom and I. My daddy has to stay in the city and work.'

Mickey, who knew exactly what type of work Mr Swanson specialised in when his wife was not looking, offered a smiling acceptance. 'I'm glad I ran into you,' she said. 'We're planning a blueberrying trip for tomorrow. Care to come?'

'First tell me who that beautiful man is you're walking out with.'

'Beautiful? Harry?' And that's another strange statement, Mickey told herself. Homely rather than beautiful.

'The guy driving the car up this way,' Sue Ellen commented. 'Him.' Her index finger pointed.

'Oh, him,' Come into my parlour, Mickey thought. Everything's working just right! 'That's my brother, Harry!'

'Is he coming tomorrow?'

'I don't know. I haven't asked him.'

'If he's coming, I'm coming,' Sue Ellen giggled. 'Even thought I hate swamps and mosquitoes—and blueberries. What time?'

'Nine o'clock, at the Pavilion landing?'

'That sounds good to me. What do I bring?'

'A sunhat, a bucket, and a big smile?'

'I guess I could manage that. But I'm not leaving here without an introduction, Mickey!'

Harry brought the car to a gentle stop by the porch of the market, and unfolded himself from the bucket seat. A smile twitched at the corners of his mouth as he came up to the two girls. 'Another lovely friend, Mike?'

'Well, of course,' she said firmly. 'I have lots of friends.'

'Of course you do,' he acknowledged. Mickey stared at him, unable to tell whether or not there was a touch of sarcasm in it all. He took advantage of her distraction by thrusting his hand out at Sue Ellen. 'I'm Harry Butterworth,' he said, laughing. 'Lawyer, fence-mender, and all-round do-gooder.' He stopped for a second, rocking back and forth on his heels, openly laughing. 'And, for my sins, Mickey's brother.'

'How lucky,' Sue Ellen gasped.

'Me?'

'She means me,' Mickey snapped. 'He's my brother, Sue, but he's also an all-round lady's man. I wouldn't trust him——'

'Further than she can throw her piano,' he finished the statement for her, and then beamed a very self-satisfied smile at both of them. Like a benediction, Mickey thought angrily. And there's Sue Ellen, eating it all up! But isn't that just what I wanted of her? So how come I'm so darned mad? I seem to be having trouble counting all my marbles these past two days. Now if I can just settle down, and——

'We were talking about tomorrow, Harry,' she said.

'Were you indeed,' he answered cautiously. And then, like a swimmer putting a toe in the cold water, 'What about tomorrow?'

'Mickey and I are going out for blueberries,' Sue Ellen trilled. 'But it certainly would be better if there were a man along. Sometimes going into those swamps around the lake can be very dangerous, you know.'

My God, Mickey thought, another one doing it! The next thing she'll do is fall down and kiss his foot! Isn't that sickening?

'It sounds like a wonderful idea,' Harry said. 'Blueberries. I wonder what it is I've forgotten about blueberries. Mickey?'

'Don't ask me,' she said stiffly. 'I'm not your memory.' And then, almost grudgingly, 'Do you want to come along?'

'How could I resist such a gracious invitation,' he returned. 'Of course I'll come along. I suppose I get to row the boat?'

'We have an outboard motor,' she muttered. 'And we'd better get these groceries home before the frozen stuff isn't.'

'Isn't what?'

'Isn't frozen any more.'

He had a few dozen pleasantries to exchange with Sue Ellen. Mickey fumed as she stacked the groceries in the boot. Thank God, she told herself, George and I aren't that way. What nonsense they're talking! With George, things are just so—comfortable.

'All the work done?' He was right behind her, at her ear again. The ear, and every other part of her, tingled.

'Yes.' She gritted her teeth to keep too many other words from following, but some escaped. 'Thank you for your help.'

'My goodness. Sarcasm.' He grinned at her. 'And I thought you would appreciate my taking an interest in Sue Ellen.'

I do, I do, her reasoning mind insisted, but all she could get past her knotted tongue was a grunt.

The drive back to the house was slow. 'I don't want to break the eggs,' he explained. He didn't explain why one free arm was around her shoulders, pulling her over on the seat until they were so close a jack of hearts couldn't squeeze in between them. She mulled that one over in her mind as she sat up stiffly, and warily watched every movement of his hands. The jack of hearts might not fit, but the joker?

The thought hit her like a tiny spark of electricity. Gently, trying hard to appear as if nothing was happening, she squirmed away from him, until she was on the outmost edge of the seat. A smile flashed across his solemn face. It became almost a grin as he pulled up in front of the house.

She made a move towards the door, but stopped under his hand.

'This expedition tomorrow,' he mused. 'I wonder why it starts at the Pavilion dock instead of right here in front of the house? We have a perfectly good dock, the boats are here already, and we're a good half-mile closer to the best blueberry bushes than we would be going all the way across the cove to town. So why is that, do you suppose?'

She made one more feeble effort to get out, but the gentle hand became a steel band, holding her back. Turning her round, in fact, so that she had to face him. 'Is my little sister up to something?'

'No, I'm not,' she denied angrily. 'Just because you have a law degree doesn't give you the right to cross-examine me on everything I do or say! Turn me loose, Harry.'

'Just as soon as I get an answer,' he promised smoothly. She struggled for another moment or two, knowing that the look on his face told the whole story. There was no way in this world he was going to turn her loose without an answer. That being the case, she scrambled for the best lie she could concoct. It was hardly stated before it was condemned.

'You don't expect me to believe that garbage, do you? You want to keep things quiet so Dad can have his rest? Baloney, Mickey. Now, the truth, please.'

She glared at him, gaining another second or two by tightening the loose braid in her hair, then leaving it to fall in all its softness down over her breast. It was impossible to meet his eyes. 'Harry, you wouldn't believe it,' she started off, her voice barely above a whisper.

'Sure I would. Try me.'

'Papa Gregory——' A pause to make sure the right words would come out. 'Your father—he doesn't like George worth a nickel. He roared at me, Harry. He's never done that before. He said something like, "The man's an out-and-out rascal, and I won't have him on the property!" I don't understand how he can be so prejudiced. George is a fine man—even you must have noticed how good-looking he is?' There was a touch of wistfulness to the tail of the sentence.

'Yes,' he said, almost whispering, to match her tone and level. 'You brought him round and Papa roared at you, and that made you all the more determined to marry the man, didn't it?'

'Yes,' she sighed. 'I really—love him a great deal, Harry.'

'Of course you do, love. I imagine he's the first man you've ever fallen in love with?'

'Oh, no! There's you and your father, and—I don't remember the rest. But there were three or four others.' A defiant statement. He's not going to confuse me, she thought fiercely. It's not puppy love. It's not!

'But you don't remember their names—these other men?'

'I—no. They've gone completely out of my mind. Isn't that what you would expect, now that George has come along?'

'Hey, we're getting altogether too serious,' he chuckled. 'I don't know much about the subject. They don't teach that sort of thing in law school.'

'But you've known so many women, Harry!'

'That doesn't mean I learned anything,' he said wryly.

'But you would help me, wouldn't you?'

'In anything, Mike. What is it you want me to do?'

She thought about it carefully. Measuring words with Harry often led into strange endings, as she knew to her regret. 'What I want you to do,' she said slowly, 'is to help make Papa Gregory happy about my wedding.'

He thought that over for a moment. 'Yes, that sounds like something I could do,' he returned. 'But in my own way, right?'

The load lifted from her mind instantly. She leaned over and kissed his cheek. 'Of course,' she said happily. 'I knew you would see it that way.'

He patted her cheek gently. 'Have I ever let you down before?'

'Never,' she giggled, her cup running over. She flipped the door open and swung her feet out on to the ground.

'Hey,' he yelled at her disappearing back. 'What about the groceries?'

'That's what big brothers are for,' she returned, offering him a gamine grin over her shoulder before she closed the screen door behind her.

CHAPTER THREE

THE morning was ideal for Mickey's expedition. The sun shone, and a few high white billowing clouds offered occasional relief. The wind was just heavy enough to ripple the surface of the lake. She stood on the family dock, shaking with enthusiasm and expectation, checking supplies. The wind tugged at the long sleeves of her simple red cotton blouse. She made an extra effort to tuck the tails into her new blue jeans, and settled her wide-brimmed straw hat more firmly on her head. Nothing glamorous, but then blueberrying was not a glamorous trade. Her only concession to fashion was the single late-blooming daffodil she had picked just outside the kitchen door, and tucked under the blue band of her hat.

Food for four—and drink. She checked everything off on her mental list. Baskets for the berry gathering, and the polyethylene icebox. Extra shoes for herself, suntan lotion, a wide-brimmed hat. The first aid box was tucked away in the bow of the big rubber pontoon-boat, a stack of life-jackets huddled under the stern thwart next to the batteries, and all she needed was one very slow brother.

'I don't see how you can drink so much coffee,' she had snapped at him over the breakfast table. 'You'll have to find a bathroom before we get out of sight of land!'

He had looked up at her lazily, that huge grin spreading across his face. 'I hate to be hurried,' he had said. 'You must

49

remember that. Don't hurry Harry. That's the watchword in these parts.'

'Well, we'll be——' She had stopped short. Papa Gregory was looking at her with those questioning eyes, and she didn't want him to know that they would be picking up others.

Harry had chuckled at her confusion. 'And besides, I want to have a word or two with my father.' And what could a girl say to something like that? She had snatched up her sunglasses and stomped out of the house.

It had hardly taken the width of the veranda for her to cool down. She had berated herself all the rest of the way down to the dock. 'He's only trying to get at you,' she warned herself disgustedly. 'And every time you fly up in a rage, he laughs. Doesn't that tell you something, dunderhead?'

'Never trust a girl who talks to herself, that's what it tells me.' She whirled on him, anger heightened by frustration, her face strawberry red.

'You—you *sneaker-up,*' she stammered, pounding on his chest with her fists. 'Any nice person would have made a noise—squeaked a plank, or something!'

'Squeaked a plank?' He hardly waited for an answer, but took her arm and hurried her into the boat. 'So, I really don't have to row? I thought outboard motors were banned to keep the lake pure?'

'It was just a local agreement, not a law,' she snapped. 'And besides, that's an electric motor. The batteries are under the life-jackets.'

'Fully charged, of course?'

She slipped out of her shoes and came across the wobbly boat to stand directly in front of him, hands on hips. 'Why do you have to act as if I were your idiot relative?' she asked angrily. 'All you ever do is try to put me down, Harry, and I don't like that the tiniest bit!'

His smile disappeared as he tilted her chin up with one finger. 'It's a bad habit I got into in my misspent childhood,' he said sombrely, 'and something I continued as a defence mechanism. If I apologise prettily, will you forgive me?'

It was too much for her. His head tilted slightly, the corners of his mouth turned up, his hair ruffled by wind and movement—it all contributed to that 'little boy lost' look that he had always used against her. She had no defence. To stifle the giggles she threw her arms around him and hung on. 'You're a fool, Harry Butterworth,' she gurgled, 'and I love you with all my heart.'

'We'll see about that,' he returned with a chuckle. 'After I see what you've brought for lunch. Shove off—or whatever it is they say.'

'Not so fast,' she muttered. 'I forgot the canoe.' It was part of the scheme, and she had no intention of explaining in that vein. Brother Harry was altogether too keen to miss a clue like that. But he asked anyway.

'Canoe? This darned rubber boat will hold eight comfortably. Why do we need a canoe?'

'Because——' she muttered, hopping back on to the dock to secure the painter of the light aluminium craft. 'Catch. And watch where you tie it. I don't want the line too near the outboard motor!'

'So now who's the idiot?' She smiled down at him, and stepped back into the boat. The electric motor eased power to the propeller almost noiselessly, and the ungainly convoy headed out across the cove. He sat in the stern, steering. There was room beside him, but she cuddled herself up on the thwart in front of him, and stared her fill.

Half-way across the cove he took his eyes off the course they were following and measured her up and down very thoroughly. 'Something wrong?' she asked. 'Did I not get my hair combed or something?'

'Just looking,' he laughed. 'Cats and queens. That sort of thing.'

She took a deep breath to steady herself. 'Oh, Harry,' she sighed. 'I did so miss you. So very much.'

'And I you,' he said quietly. 'Your violent temper, your lovely face, that magnificent red hair, the steel in your backbone—I've missed it all, Mike.'

'Harry, I——'

'Me first,' he said. 'Age before beauty. Are you really going to marry that—what's-his-name?'

'George,' she supplied, pulling her knees up and hugging them. 'Yes, I'm really going to marry him. I promised I would, and I don't break promises.' Her grey eyes searched his face for some clue. He's up to something, she told herself. I wonder if I'll ever find out what?

'You always were a stubborn child.'

'Mule-headed, you told me then. Why are you being so nice to me?'

Harry ignored the attack. He waved in the general direction of the lake. 'This certainly beats living in Boston.' He leaned forward in her direction. The breeze from their passage was tugging at the neck of his short-sleeved shirt, showing the corded muscles of his throat. 'And his cousin—what was her name?'

'Veronica.'

'Yeah, Veronica. Known her long?'

'Only a couple of weeks,' she sighed. 'She's really not

your type, Harry.'

'Not my type? Now you're an expert on my likes and dislikes?'

'I—no. I'm sorry, I shouldn't have said that.'

'Probably not,' he chuckled, 'but it never stopped you before. What's this all about?'

'I don't know, Harry. I just don't want to fight with you any more. I don't know why.'

'No, of course you don't.' All seriousness now, he moved forward and teased her hair with a solid finger. 'And you do keep your promises. An admirable trait. Just tell me this, Mike. Why?'

'Why what?'

'Why did you promise to marry him?'

She whirled around to face the bow. He was too perceptive. Let him read what he could from her back. And besides, what sort of reaction would there be if she told him the truth? I'm going to marry him because my mother told me I can't have the man I fell in love with when I was fourteen. I'm going to marry him because he's the only man who's ever asked me, and I'm afraid of growing old alone!

'Hey, tears?'

'Don't be silly,' she muttered. 'It's just the—wind in my eyes. Watch out for the dock.'

Harry swung the boat gently up against the Pavilion dock as if he had been piloting lake boats for years. It wasn't really a dock, although it had the name. It was a moored raft, just inches above the level of the lake itself. And there were three people waiting.

'I just couldn't leave Veronica at home on such a day.' George reached down into the boat and pulled Mickey up. 'There's bound to be plenty of room, isn't there?'

'Of course.' Harry shut down the motor and held the boat in position by muscle power. He flashed the blonde a big smile. 'But those high heels are liable to knock a hole in the boat.' Veronica grimaced as she slipped out of her shoes and came aboard. The combination was too much, Mickey thought. Me in jeans, Sue Ellen in that wild orange thing, and now Veronica in a neat-as-a-pin striped sailor dress. The bright blue background emphasised the woman's figure; the thin white stripes kept everything from being a bit too much. The wide white sailor's collar set off her thin face to perfection. But the last thing in the world one would wear to go berry picking!

'I don't know why I came.' Sue Ellen was in a gloomy mood before the party started. Gloomy, but dressed to kill. A lightweight silk catsuit encased her volumptuous figure, but barely. It was of luminescent orange, bright enough to be seen for miles. Her dark hair gleamed in the sun. No hat, Mickey noted glumly. This is going to be some trip. She stood aside while George did the honours for Sue Ellen. Harry remained on the stern thwart. His grin was beginning to change from 'welcome' to 'wolf'. Mickey shuddered. The whole scheme was collapsing in front of her, and there was nothing she could do about it.

She dropped down into the curve of the bow as Harry cast off. The boat nosed out into the open lake, and began its slow progression northwards past the chain of tiny islands that were spotted at random down the middle of the lake. Veronica, after initial reconnaissance, managed to squeeze herself in at the stern with Harry. Sue Ellen took the seat that Mickey had abandoned and stared hungrily sternwards. To make matters worse, George squeezed himself in beside Mickey. Now why did I think of it that way? she asked herself. Guilt made her respond more than she might ordinarily have done.

She wiggled until George's hip was hard up against her own, and his arm went around her shoulders. There was no place for her head to go except against his chest, and she went into that nest with a little sigh. It might even have sounded like pleasure. At least George thought so. The arm around her shoulders tightened and the hand moved downwards. She stopped its further advance by holding it locked against her shoulder-blade. One peep out from under her long eyelashes showed Harry at his entertaining best, but every time his gaze crossed hers there was murder in his eyes. Mickey shuddered again. Lord knew what George must have thought. He brought up his other arm and cradled her against him while his lips nuzzled at her forehead.

The lake was long and wide, but not by any means the largest of the more than one thousand stretches of water in the Adirondack park. The little electric motor puttered enthusiastically, but it took a full hour for them to reach the mouth of the Canastago River, where low swamp lands made ideal sites for blueberry bushes. The river earned its title purely from custom; in any other place it would have been called a brook. Two hundred yards out from its mouth was tiny Pachcaog island, a brush-laden hump of earth that barely cleared the water by ten feet at its highest point.

Harry slowed the motor and they drifted by. Time to put the plan in motion, Mickey told herself. 'Look, there are too many of us for one site, Harry. Why don't you take Sue Ellen and go over to the island in the canoe? The rest of us can work from the boat over in the swamps.'

'Ah,' he chuckled. She waited for something more, but it

didn't come from Harry.

'I do believe I'll go to the island, too,' Veronica stated, and then looked to see if someone was going to challenge her decision. 'I really hate little boats, and this—thing—hardly rates the name.'

'Well, I'm going with Harry, too,' Sue Ellen insisted. Harry looked down the length of the boat at Mickey and shrugged his shoulders. He did not appear to be absolutely devastated by the idea. It hardly fitted into Mickey's plans. Before she could re-arrange her thoughts she was attacked from the other side.

'Since there are three of us going to the island,' Veronica said, 'I think it's only fair that you and George should take the canoe, while we take the boat with us.'

'That would be fun,' George contributed. Mickey looked up at him. Her betrothed had a different kind of fun in mind than she did.

'It's hard to pick berries from a canoe,' she grumbled. 'And you know you don't—oh, what the devil. All right.'

Another ten minutes were required, redistributing the load between boat and canoe, transferring passengers, and establishing rendezvous points for later. When the boat finally chugged triumphantly away, Mickey, in the stern of the canoe, shook her head in disgust. Things were definitely not going her way. And now there was George to deal with.

'Paddle us over there,' she pointed. 'There's a break in the underbrush, and it looks as if there are berries there. Over there, where that grove of willows stands.' She gestured, rocking the canoe. George grabbed for both sides of the craft.

'Easy,' he called. There was a very unhappy sound to his voice. And then, 'I don't have a paddle.'

'I've got one. You can take it.'

'I can't paddle from the bow,' he snapped. 'You have to paddle a canoe from the stern.'

'So we'll change places.' She started to get up, and the canoe rocked madly.

'Don't do that,' he yelled. 'Dear God, you'll have us in the lake in no time. Where are the life-jackets?'

'On the boat,' she sighed. 'Don't be difficult, George. Am I supposed to paddle?'

'Women's liberation,' he muttered. 'Let's get over on dry land.'

'That isn't exactly dry land,' she grated, dipping the paddle into the water. This isn't the way it's supposed to go at all, she told herself grimly. When she put her back to it, the tiny canoe fairly jumped out of the water, and before she was aware the nose of the little craft rammed up on to a tiny bit of beach.

'Now that's more like it,' George said. 'Why don't we just sit over here under the trees for a while? It's hot out on the water.'

'I'll bet it must be,' she sighed. He pulled the canoe up out of the water, and took her hand. 'The baskets,' she reminded him.

'They can wait,' he chuckled, 'and I can't. Do you realise that this is the first time I've had you alone in over a month?'

'Has it been that long?' There was no room for argument. He towed her along in his wake and deposited her with a bump in the nest of grass at the foot of the biggest tree. It towered above her head a full fifty feet, its grey bark resinous.

'Yeah, it's been that long.' He was down beside her before she could move—almost on top of her, to be exact.

Oh, me, she thought. I hadn't thought! And she hadn't.
Since his proposal over a month ago she had been too busy
with Papa Gregory to sit down and think. Marriage had
been the in thing. One thought of long white dresses and
receptions and happily-ever-after, and she had given little
thought to what happened between 'happily' and 'after'.
And here she was, practically alone with George, who was
looking for an advance payment.

'Look at that hawk,' she improvised, shifting away from
him.

'Yeah, hawk,' he grumbled. 'For God's sake, hold still.'

It was an unfortunate time for her ingrained honesty to
come waltzing to the fore. You owe him something, she told
herself. Not everything, but something! It took a moment to
school her senses, but she managed, turning a smiling face
to him, and moved closer. He had a face of remarkable male
beauty—seen from a distance. Close up all the little bumps
and furrows that made up the big picture were
disillusioning. But it's too late for that, she told herself, and
closed her eyes.

His lips came down on hers in practised warmth. Gently
at first, and then more demanding. She did her best to
respond. There had been plenty of response a month
before, but now something was different. Mickey didn't
know what it was, and didn't want that difference to be, but
it was there.

Feeling her lack of response, George pressed harder,
demandingly. She parted her lips under his urging, and
almost clinically measured her own response to his questing
tongue. Nothing. But it was only on her side of the lips that
passion lacked. George was breathing in short desperate
gasps as his hand fumbled for the buttons on her blouse.

Her hand made a gesture of protest, but she restrained the movement. He did deserve something. He was almost frantic as he broke the strap of her bra and cupped her small firm breast.

'Oh, God,' he muttered, fumbling with the remainder of her buttons, baring her to the waist. Feel something, she roared at herself. His hand is clammy, her body replied. You're not trying, her mind interjected. His teeth nipped at the bronze peak of her breast.

'You're hurting me,' she complained in a low trembling voice. He continued with his meal. 'George, you're hurting me!' It wasn't a terrible pain. Not half as terrible as the thought that came crashing through her mind. God, this is the man that I'm going to marry!

He pulled away from her reluctantly. 'What's the matter?'

'I don't know. Maybe I'm tired.' She did her best to re-arrange her clothes. 'Maybe I—maybe we'd better pick some berries.'

'Berries hell!' he muttered, still breathing hard. She wiggled away from him and got up, brushing down her jeans. 'You mean you really want to pick berries?'

'Well, it wouldn't look right if we didn't come back with something,' she said. He was looking up at her in disgust.

'I'd love to come back with something,' he grumbled, 'but not berries, lady. We're going to be married in a month. Doesn't that mean something?'

'Yes,' she almost cried, 'but not what you're thinking, George. I don't want to give samples. Don't spoil my day, please.'

'So pick your damned berries,' he snarled. 'I'll sit right here and watch.' She glared down at him until her conscience bothered her, and then snatched up one of the straw-woven baskets and headed into the bushes.

It was hot work, locked away from the breezes by the swamp growth, struggling from bush to bush, but she did manage to fill her container. The bushes seemed to be snatching at her, refusing to let her go. She struggled, accumulating more than one scratch on the way, hurrying to get back to George. She had worried at him in her mind as a dog worries a bone. He had asked her to marry him; she had accepted. Betrothed, even if hardly anyone else knew it. And she had treated him too cruelly for kindness. So he had gone further than ever before, made more blatant sexual moves than she was prepared for. Could that be such a crime, a month before their wedding day? It's my fault, she finally concluded. I wasn't prepared to go that extra mile, and I should have.

The conclusion was neat, well-packaged, and just the sort of thing a sensible girl ought to arrive at. So why doesn't it seem to fit, she asked herself as she burst out of the thicket, ready to explain it all. She might just as well have taken her time. George was fast asleep. Her wry grin was for herself, not for him. Walking softly to avoid wakening him, she went down to the canoe and stowed her basket of berries. He was still asleep as she cleared up all the other paraphernalia. Since she couldn't explain, she did the next best thing, lying down beside him, curling up against him, and gently pulling his hand over until it cupped her breast. And promptly went to sleep.

The scream woke them both. 'What on earth——' George managed as he struggled up to a sitting position. Jarred by his movement, Mickey sat up as well.

'Bobcat?' she suggested.

'Not likely this close,' he assessed. 'There it goes again.'

'My God, it's someone on the island!' she gasped. 'One of the girls. Come on, George!' She was up and running before he could make up his mind to move, and had the canoe in the water before he lumbered up. It surprised her. George was a graceful man, good at most sports, fluid. But this was the first time she had seen him just as he was waking up. She stored the thought away, realising how very little she really knew about her man.

'Get in,' he commanded. 'I'll paddle.'

It wasn't the sort of thing she was accustomed to. She usually made decisions for herself, but George needed to be pandered to. She gave him what she hoped was a submissive smile and climbed into the bow. He was behind her quickly, using the paddle as a punting pole to push them clear of the swampy underbrush. The scream sounded one more time. George, proficient with the paddle, moved them out into the lake at flank speed.

'There, just off the port side,' she called back. 'I don't know what's going on. The boat is out there, drifting.'

'Maybe,' George grunted, 'but the screaming is coming from the island.' He put his back to it again, and the distance closed between the two craft.

'There's nobody aboard,' she said softly as they came alongside. 'What do you—don't do that, George!'

'Don't do what?' He had put his paddle aside, and was trying to stand up in the tiny aluminium canoe.

'Don't do *that*,' she yelled as the narrow craft rocked violently. He made a desperate move to regain balance, and failed. The canoe went over in the opposite direction from the rubber boat, and they both hit the water. The sudden bath meant little to Mickey. She had grown up by the lake,

a true water-baby. Only one regret struck her mind as she
dived deep, under the canoe and up the other side. All those
blueberries, so laboriously picked!

Her head broke the surface between the overturned canoe
and the empty rubber boat. There was little choice; she
picked the boat because it was more stable. A moment of
struggle and she came up over its side on her stomach, and
slid down into the well. She held the position for a second
or two, then curled into a ball and came up on her knees,
brushing her long hair back from her face. Another scream
echoed from the island. Mickey stood up in the boat and
shaded her eyes, but could see nothing.

For a moment she could not remember what she was
looking for, and then it struck her. George. Where in God's
name was George? She scrabbled along the side of the boat,
and saw nothing. The overturned canoe bobbed alongside,
and she heard a strangled moan. There was no way she
could scramble across the canoe to get a better view.
Without pausing any further she pushed her hair back and
dived in over the bow.

Four easy strokes took her around to the other side of the
canoe. George was there, hanging on desperately with one
hand. She powered her way up to him. He was almost
unconscious. A knot was forming on the side of his head,
and a trickle of blood oozed from a small cut above the eye.
'Hit my head on the side of the canoe,' he muttered
groggily.

His hand was slipping. She ducked under and came up
beneath his arm, using her own treading motions to keep
him afloat. His other hand grabbed at her shoulder, almost
pushing her under. She blew water out of her nose and
mouth, and made a quick assessment. The tiny canoe was of

no help. There was no real handholds, and the climb up on top of its keel was too much for her to handle. Warily, one move at a time, she began to propel them around the canoe in the direction of the rubber boat.

Here there was some help. A small line was rigged around the perimeter of the boat for just such need. She snatched at it, completely exhausted, then wrapped George's hands around it.

Her fiancé was still groggy, but not out of control. She checked his position in the water, then dragged herself up into the well of the craft, and collapsed. What to do now? When in doubt, her mother always said, scream. She filled her lungs with all the air they could hold, and turned loose a wild roar of a scream that frightened half the birds in the area. She heard a splash in the distance, but had her head down, searching the bottom of the boat for something—some tool—to help her complete the rescue. George was fully conscious, saying a large number of short fat words that she had thought appeared only in pornographic books. He graduated from short words to longer ones. Imprecaution. Threats. Anguish.

Discarding her first idea, Mickey came up to her knees and bent over the side of the boat, struggling for George's hands. It was no easy work for a girl, especially one her size. She gritted her teeth and pulled, rocking the boat but not moving George an inch. She was concentrating so hard that the sudden tug and dip from the back of the craft came as a complete surprise. Harry, who had been swimming across from the island at life-saver speed, had just porpoised into the boat.

'Dear God,' he yelled as he threw himself on top of her. 'Mickey! Are you all right? You scared the hell out of me!'

'Well I was all right until you jumped on me,' she groaned. 'What's——'

'I don't know what,' he growled, 'What were you yelling for? I don't see any blood.'

'Not me,' she protested. 'George. He's over the side—and he's hurt. What's all the hollering on the island?'

'You wouldn't believe,' he snarled. 'Where is this—Lothario of yours?'

'Over the side,' she muttered. 'I was holding his hands. I think you broke my rib or something.'

'I'll break more than that one day,' he gritted through clenched lips. He set her aside, none too gently, and stretched a hand down to the man in the water.

'So climb in,' Harry invited sarcastically. 'We don't have time for another swimming lesson today.'

George coughed to clear his throat, but made no move to come aboard.

'Come on,' Harry yelled at him. 'I've got two more crazies to take care of.'

'I can't,' George returned. 'I—just can't.'

'What the devil,' Harry snarled. He lowered himself gingerly over the side, managed to get behind George, and gave him a shove upward. Mickey grabbed at George's hands and pulled. One more shove from behind sent the blond man sprawling into the boat. Harry vaulted in behind him.

'Grab the painter of the canoe,' he ordered as he made his way to the stern.

'Since there aren't any other slaves in sight, I suppose you mean me,' Mickey muttered.

'Look,' Harry snarled, 'I just saved your financé's life——'

'Huh!' Mickey snorted. 'In another five minutes I would

have had him aboard by myself.'

'One more crack like that and I'll have you over my knee,' Harry growled. 'Did you think I swam all the way out here just to save *him*?' Mickey's head snapped up and her eyes locked on him as he started the little electric motor. It would have been nice if he had volunteered the rest of the statement, but he wasn't going to, and she was too proud to ask, Why did you swim all the way out here, Harry? For some reason anger was growing, choking her.

'There wasn't any need,' she growled at him. 'I'm a champion swimmer. I got more trophies than you did, wise guy.'

'Yeah, in the children's division,' he grunted. 'Shut up and let me concentrate, will you? Tend to Lothario, there. He seems to have swallowed a great deal of water.'

'Harry Butterworth,' she snapped, 'you are the most unfeeling darned—brother—that a girl ever had!'

'Probably,' he grunted. 'Where did that other idiot go to?'

Mickey refused to rise to the bait. She dropped to her knees and cradled George's head against her breast. No doubt about it, she told herself fiercely, I made the right choice. George appreciates me! She smoothed the blond hair from his face and kissed him gently on the forehead. The man in the stern of the boat made a very rude noise, but before she could retaliate the boat scraped bottom on the sandy beach of the island, and Harry was up and gone.

She followed slowly, helping George to a dry hillock under a majestic white oak tree, and going back to be sure of the boat's mooring. Then curiosity caught up with the cat.

'Hey, don't leave me alone,' George called after her anxiously.

'You'll be OK, love,' she promised. 'I want to help out.'

The path up to the centre of the island was as familiar as her own veranda. Papa Gregory had always loved to come here, and fishing had once been good at this end of the lake. Half-way up the slope she came across Veronica, sitting with her back against a small spruce tree, looking daggers at the world, and soaking wet. All the sophistication had gone out of her dress; it was a mass of wrinkles. Her high-heeled shoes had almost disintegrated, and her hair sprawled in several directions at once.

Mickey dropped down on one knee at her side. 'What happened? Are you hurt?'

'No, I'm not hurt,' the other woman grumbled. 'He didn't even stop to ask.'

'No manners,' Mickey retorted. 'Never had any, never will have any. I know he's my brother, but he's a thoroughly disreputable man.' And if God doesn't strike me dead on the spot for such lies I'll be forever grateful!

'Well, there's no need for you to sit there and stare,' Veronica said gracelessly. 'Where's George?'

'Down by the boat landing,' Mickey said. 'What happened?'

'What happened!' Veronica lost all her control, and started to yell. 'I was bored to death, that's what happened, and I decided to go home, and that—that damned boat—I couldn't get the motor started, and then I fell off, and that brother of yours stood there and laughed.' Realising how much of herself she was giving away, the woman took a deep breath and regained control of herself.

'I'm sure he was coming to help me,' she continued softly, 'when that idiot woman started screaming. And after that——Where are you going?'

'I forgot the other idiot,' Mickey exclaimed, and

was off up the path as quickly as her legs could carry her. At the very top of the tiny mound that was called a hill was another white oak tree. Hoary with age, decorated with moss, it towered a good sixty feet upward. Harry was leaning against its base, shaking his head; Sue Ellen Swanson was perched six feet up in the air on one of the branches. Mickey slowed to a saunter. All her clever scheme lay smashed around her feet. There was obviously no dire emergency before her. The two of them, one at the foot of the tree, the other in the branches, were exchanging glares the like of which brought the first shots at Fort Sumter in the Civil War. Walk more slowly, she told herself. And think, for goodness' sake. See what can be salvaged.

A little soothing seemed to be in order. 'Thank you, Harry——'

'For what?' he grumbled.

'For saving my life,' she said sweetly.

'Huh! Tell your idiot friend to come down.'

'Harry! She has a name.'

'You bet she has,' he snarled. 'I just used it.'

She could feel that ripple of anger rising in herself again. It had no rhyme or reason; if just seemed to explode to the surface. She struggled to control it, and barely managed to do so. 'Sue Ellen?' she called.

'I'm not coming down until that snake is gone.' the girl in the tree said. Her voice had lost the overlay of her Vassar training. All her Alabama accent was on full display.

'Snake? What snake, Harry?'

'That vicious one over there,' he grunted. 'I told her, but she wouldn't believe me. I doubt she would come down for me if I sang three verses of "Dixie" and flew the Confederate flag.'

'Children! Both of you,' Mickey grumbled. She walked over to the bush where he had pointed. A three foot black-bodied snake was thrashing around in the grass with a cluster of young sprawling over it. Three yellow stripes ran down the long body. Mickey shook her head slowly and walked back to the base of the tree.

'Sue Ellen! Come down this instant. It's only a garter snake. It couldn't hurt you if it tried.'

'Well, it tried,' Sue Ellen quavered. 'Are you sure it's not poisonous?'

'I'm sure,' Mickey promised. 'Come on down, dear.' It must have been the soft assurance that did it. The girl up in the tree began to make her way slowly down through the branches, dropping the last few feet into Harry's arms.

Harry carried Sue Ellen down the trail to the boat landing, where the rest of the bedraggled expedition was waiting. George's face was flushed, as if his cousin had been giving him some straight truths. Mickey walked over to his side and examined the bump on his forehead. The cut was still bleeding. She climbed back into the boat and fished out the first aid kit. There was nothing she knew to do except put on a compression bandage, and hope the bleeding would stop. George was too belligerent to thank her for the effort.

It's pride, she told herself, more than injury. I made him look like some sort of fool, and his pride has been injured. I suppose I'll have to spend a week being a submissive little thing to get back into his good graces. But I *want* to. We're going to be married! She dropped down to her knees in front of him and let body language tell him how sorry she was.

'Now,' Harry muttered,' do you suppose we could get this expedition back to the base before I have a nervous breakdown?'

CHAPTER FOUR

PAPA GREGORY was feeling the devil in him. Mickey could see it plainly on his face. The three Butterworths had, by some strange alchemy, managed to avoid each other for the remainder of that dismal expedition day, but now, at lunch the next day, there was nowhere to hide.

Harry slumped in his chair, toying with the fish chowder. Papa Gregory was spooning his up with great enthusiasm. Mickey had served them both, then pulled out her own chair. It's truly family, she sighed to herself. Nobody offered to help!

'So, how many blueberries did you get?' Papa, throwing the first dart. Harry almost choked over his chowder. Mickey ducked her head, fussing with her napkin. 'Well?'

'I picked a couple of quarts,' she offered hesitantly, wishing that she could vanish from the table.

'So we'll have blueberry pie tonight?'

'I—no,' she confessed. 'I didn't bring them home.'

'Oh?' Her stepfather leaned forward, one elbow on the table, and a look of teasing interest on his face. Torquemada, judging the heretics, she thought to herself. Bring the guilty rascal in and we'll give him a fair trial—before we hang him. Her. But she hadn't done anything wrong. Clumsy, perhaps, but not wrong! She stuck out her little Devlin chin.

'They were in the canoe,' she muttered. 'It capsized. We lost all the berries—and the basket, too, come to think of it. My favourite basket.'

69

'And damn near lost her fiancé,' Harry joined in. 'Can you imagine that? The great athlete can't swim!'

Oh, Harry, he can, too, she screamed to herself. I wish you hadn't said that. Not about the canoe; just that word—fiancé! I wish you hadn't said that. She lifted her head just far enough to see Papa Gregory across the table. By now, according to all the past experience Mickey had had over George, he should be turning mottled blue and red in the face, ready to hurl a few thunderbolts in her general direction.

Instead, the old man was smiling. Actually smiling! She stole a quick glance at Harry. His head was down, eyes following his spoon, but the corners of his lips were turned up—a dead giveaway. Whatever had happened to bring Gregory's smile had been Harry's doing. She knew it—but wasn't sure whether to thank him or beat him up. Or maybe both!

'Try smiling, girl.' She looked up at her stepfather and managed a very weak smile. Very weak indeed.

Papa Gregory laid his napkin aside. 'Good chowder,' he acknowledged. 'Pay attention, Harry. This girl can cook up a storm.' He shifted in his chair to get comfortable. 'My son, the lawyer,' he started out, with just a touch of sarcasm from one who had been on the bench for twenty years, 'has convinced me—almost—that I have it all wrong about young George Armstead.'

Mickey, who had been holding her breath, let it all out in a massive sigh.

'Understand, I have to be convinced,' Papa Gregory continued. 'You should bring him around so I can check him out.' And then, more sharply, 'I'd be disappointed if you married without approval, Michele. It's your right, of course, but I'd be disappointed.'

'I—I wish you wouldn't ask that, Papa,' she told him wistfully. 'It's so hard when someone wants you to make a choice between the people you love. Sometimes I think things are never—I mean—I wish you wouldn't ask. I don't *mean* to be a disappointment to you, but a girl is entitled to make her own mistakes.'

'I understand,' the old man said gruffly, and stabbed at one eye with his napkin. 'You must do as you see fit, love, not what *I* want.'

'Do what your mama would want,' Harry interjected. It was a low blow. Papa's statement was clear-cut; Harry's was threatening her with memories and commitments. She shivered under the weight of it all.

'Pay him no attention, there's a good girl,' the old man commented. 'So much like your mother, Michele. Now, since *my son, the lawyer*——' laughter ran behind the phrase this time '—is determined to teach me how to fish later this afternoon, I suppose I'd better get my nap.' He rumbled out of the room with a snappier step than Mickey had seen in many a day. A moment of silence followed at the table.

'You don't have to eat the chowder if you don't like it, Harry.'

'I like it. And for goodness' sake get that mournful tone out of your voice. Even if I didn't like it I wouldn't dare not finish the plate. The biscuits are good, too. Yours?'

'Me and the packaged mix,' she giggled. And then more seriously, softly, 'I—want to thank you for helping about George.'

'I said I would,' he returned. 'And I'll always keep my promise to you, Mike.'

'You always have,' she said, perplexed. 'But somehow they don't always seem to come out the way I expect them to.

You're not—playing some game, Harry?'

'You think I would?' All the world of injured innocence was crammed into that sentence. She stared at him, unblinking. It had been one of her childhood beliefs that Harry could turn the tables on her in the wink of an eye. So then if she didn't wink, he had to be true! The sheer nonsense of the logic brought another chuckle.

'Yes, I think you would if I weren't watching out!' She was up in her chair and around the table before he could swallow the last spoonful of chowder. Both hands went around his neck in a desperate hug as she cradled his head against her breasts. 'Oh, it's so wonderful to have you home.'

'That's great,' he rumbled,' but you're choking me to death! Help!'

'Oh, stop it, you big sissy,' she gurgled. She ruffled his hair with an old familiar gesture, then stopped to look at what her hand was doing. 'Harry,' she said, aghast, 'there—there's a white hair, right there. Shall I——'

'Don't you dare pull it out,' he laughed. 'In a few years I may need that. My grandfather was as bald as a billiard ball. If you feel I deserve a reward—which I do—you can kiss me.'

It was an old line—one they had used for years together. One which would normally bring her to plant an enthusiastic smack on his forehead. But things were different now. She was suddenly embarrassed, wanting to offer the old reward, and too shy to do so. He grinned up at her, reading her mind.

'You've just grown up, Mickey,' he said.

'Nonsense,' she said determinedly. 'You saw me last Christmas, being Papa's hostess at the ball in Albany. I was certainly grown up then.'

'Not true,' he offered. 'You were still a little girl, playing at being grown up. Now, all scruffy as you are, you're definitely a woman. I'm glad. I've been waiting for that.'

'I don't know what you mean,' she sighed. 'Sometimes you talk just to confuse me, Harry.'

'Of course, Mike. You don't know what I mean—yet. But keep that in the back of your mind. Right now there's something else we need to discuss. Come on out to the porch.'

'The dishes, Harry. They won't go away, and there isn't any maid to come in and do them.'

'So I'll make you a promise,' he chuckled, taking hold of her wrist and towing her out the door. 'Unless something else comes up, after we have our little talk I'll help you do the dishes. Bargain?'

She turned the whole idea over in her very suspicious mind, and could find no loophole. 'Agreed,' she said.

He didn't actually stop on the veranda, but towed her off on to the grass and down towards the water. There was the sweet smell of balsam on the air, wafted in by an errant wind off the mountain to their back. Somewhere up on that mountain at least one balsam blister on a high-standing fir had broken, filling the air. Mickey breathed deeply. The lake was mirror-still. The tiny patch of water-lilies, the only life that had been able to resist the acid rain, rocked gently back and forth. The air sustained a hawk, drifting reverently across the blue sky, soundlessly, and a pair of plump ravens, doing their best to avoid the hawk's gaze.

'Nothing changes here,' he commented, pulling her down beside him on the edge of the grass.

'Everything changes,' she returned. 'Everything. It's not the same hawk as yesterday; the mountain is just a little smaller; the lake is—acid. And we—we've changed, Harry.'

'Oh, I know that.' He dropped back, cradling his head in his hands, swinging his right knee up over his left. 'I know the world changes, Mike, and sometimes faster than we would want. There are crisis points to which we all must come.'

'Papa Gregory? Something terrible is——He's going to die?' she asked frantically. It was all part of the dream that had bothered her for the past two weeks. Papa is fading away right in front of my eyes!

One of his hands came over to hers, and squeezed gently. 'Hey, don't get carried away. Papa has a problem, but it's not all that serious. In fact he's more worried about how to tell you about it than he is about the problem itself. You know he went into the hospital for a check-up two weeks ago? They diagnosed his difficulty as a gall-bladder problem. It's not a life-threatening thing. In fact, they have such a crowded schedule that they told him to come up here and build himself up. Dr Philbert will telephone as soon as he can schedule the operation. I can see that you're doing your part, watching his schedule, feeding him properly.'

'Oh, God, Harry. I thought—I honestly thought he——'

'I know, Mike. He just couldn't bring himself to tell you.'

'And you were appointed as bad-news bearer?'

'Wasn't I always?'

She pushed him gently back down on to the grass and leaned over on his stomach. 'Yes, you always were, Harry,' she laughed. 'But in this case no news was very bad news, and the bad news is almost good—if that makes any sense.'

'It does,' he chuckled. 'I must be slipping my mooring. Practically everything you say makes sense. It never used to be that way. Now then, we have a problem, you and I?'

'We do? I mean, do we?'

'Yes, we do.' He tapped her gently on her snub nose. 'Now pay attention. Watch my lips. We two must keep Papa in good humour for the next month. Got it?'

'I guess so. Cheer him up? Smile a lot?'

'And don't aggravate him.'

'Oh, my.'

'What's that mean?'

'He wants to meet George. I—I think maybe that might just aggravate him just the tiniest bit. Don't you?'

'Probably, but if that's what he wants, that's what he gets. You and I are going to be a great song and dance team, Mike. Nothing but light humour. Keep a stiff upper chin.'

'Lip,' she corrected automatically. 'Stiff upper lip.'

'I'll be darned if you aren't right,' he said, suddenly solemn. His two big hands trapped her face and held her locked in place as his head came up. She felt a sudden flash of fear rush through her system, followed instantly by a piercing shock as his lips gently caressed hers, paused, and came back for more. It was like nothing she had ever felt before. From the tips of her toes to the stub of her nose there was a sudden intuitive flash of femininity—a feeling that she, Mickey Devlin Butterworth, was the most wanted, most loved woman in all the world. Fire burned where his tongue touched. Nerves screamed as he withdrew. And all she could do was hang there between his hands, in awe and wonder.

He broke the spell, pushing her gently away. A small stone, hidden in the grass, scratched at her back. The incidental pain brought her out of her daze. She sat up hastily, tucking her legs under her, ducking her head to hide the guilty flush that flooded her face.

'I'm sorry, Mike.' He was sitting up beside her, one gentle hand brushing her hair out of the way so he could see her face. She took a deep breath. Song and dance, wasn't that what he had said? Play it all lightly?' I'm as good an actress as anyone in the neighbourhood!

'Sorry for what?' She forced a smile, and a little giggle. To her attentive ear it didn't sound too bad. 'No reason to be sorry, Harry. I enjoyed it very much.'

'But you don't believe it, do you?'

'Well——' There was more hesitation. He deserved an answer, but if she were honest it would be very hard. 'I—guess I didn't expect it. A girl doesn't think of her brother in—those terms.'

'Of course not,' he sighed. 'Let's talk about something else.'

'Besides keeping everything light and happy for Papa?'

'Yes. Besides that.'

'OK. How about Sue Ellen? Isn't she a sweet thing?'

'Lord, if I could have caught up with you last night, young lady, I would have whacked your bottom. Sue Ellen! Is she your candidate?'

'She's only a nice girl and a very good friend,' she answered, aggrieved. 'Candidate for what?'

'Don't give me that little Miss Innocence bit,' he laughed. 'Is she the girl you've lined up for me? Is a proposal required, or will a proposition do?'

'Me? Harry, would I do that to you?' Mickey had learned a few tricks over the years. You muster an entirely undeserved tone of righteous indignation by pinching yourself somewhere out of sight, but where it really hurt. Done properly, a girl could even work up a tear or two. As now.

Unfortunately Harry had an equal amount of experience with her little bag of tricks. She produced the grimace, the pained look, the tear, and all he did was to fall back on the grass, laughing. Which really made her angry.

'Darn you, Harry Butterworth,' she muttered. 'I could kill you. I really could.'

He sat up again, still laughing. 'I might enjoy that better

than marrying your latest little darling. Surely you could do better for me?'

'Why you—you——' Mickey almost swallowed her tongue in her haste to make several opposing statements at the same time. Stop, take four deep breaths, count up to ten, she told herself. And then glare at him.

'You know she's just your type,' she finally managed to say.

'What type is that?' Those heavy eyebrows of his were drawn in a straight line as he frowned at her.

'You know what type,' she snapped. 'She's a—nice little home body, and her father has lots of money, and——'

'I don't want to marry her father,' he drawled. 'You'll have to do better than that!'

She swallowed her anger one more time. Harry really needed a girl like Sue Ellen, and it was her responsibility to see it through. It had become a religious crusade, so to speak. 'Harry,' she said slowly, forcefully, 'she's a delightful girl, with a good many talents, and she cooks well and wants a family and talks nicely and is easy to dominate and has big boobs and——'

'And hasn't a brain in her whole head,' he interrupted lazily. 'Just my type?'

'You don't need a woman with brains,' Mickey snarled back at him. 'You always claim you're smart enough for two. Believe me, Sue Ellen is just your type! And let me tell you something, counsellor, you're not getting any younger, either!'

'So that's the way it is?' He came up to his knees and turned her to face him. 'I'm in my dotage, I suppose, and you're just bound to do me this last favour. To preserve the Butterworth name, I suppose. No, don't duck your head, girl. Let me tell you what happened out on the island.'

'I don't want to hear,' she shouted at him, and clapped her

hands over her ears.

'Well you're going to,' he shouted back at her. 'First that idiot cousin of Armstead's throws a fit about being bored, and when I'm not looking she sneaks off to the boat, gets the damned thing in the water, and then starts yelling for help because she can't start the motor. So I go after her, and naturally she falls overboard, and I have to get her back on dry land. And no sooner do I do my good deed than this other bird starts screaming. So I do my best hundred-yard dash up the hill, and what do you know—a snake has bitten her.'

'That's not possible,' Mickey said primly. 'What garter snake would bite somebody—unless you stepped on it, or fell down in the middle of the nest, or something. Did he?'

'Did he who?'

'The snake—did the snake bite her?'

'How would I know, for God's sake? By the time I got there she was already up the tree, and not willing to listen to any reasoning at all. All I could tell was she was holding on to her—a certain part of her anatomy—claiming a death wound. Did you expect me to climb the tree and peel her out of that—that——'

'Catsuit.'

'Well I didn't.'

'You must really be getting old, Harry,' she gurgled. 'That's really your kind of challenge. What stopped you?'

'You did,' he muttered. 'In the middle of all that, you started yelling.'

'And then that's when you did your Tarzan act?'

He stood up. The very act made his glare more ominous. 'For a girl who was rescued at the risk of my life, you don't seem to be very grateful,' he declared.

She stood up beside him, her glare flickering on and off as

she realised how stupid the argument had become. But from long practice, she just could not let go without the last word. 'I certainly am grateful,' she told him sweetly, 'considering that I didn't need rescuing in the first place, and you almost broke my back when you landed on top of me, and——Oh, Harry, it really was funny, wasn't it?'

'If it was, you're the only one laughing,' he said mournfully. They stared at each other, and then gradually both moved from glare to twitching mouth to outright laughter, and fell into each other's arms.

'What's going on—as if I don't know?' Papa Gregory had come out of the house and down the path. 'Is this the same argument you both started thirteen years ago?'

'Probably,' Harry remarked, pushing Mickey away from him. 'But this time it's ending differently.'

'How so?'

'You'll find it hard to believe, but Mickey has just promised to stop doing me any more favours. Isn't that true?'

With both men staring at her, she felt the return of that confusion, that shyness, that had bothered her more than once since Harry had come home. She started to turn away from both of them, but a strong masculine arm interfered. 'Isn't that true, Mickey?' There was just the hint of a threat in Harry's deep voice. Or maybe it was a promise?

'Yes,' she agreed in a husky voice. But I don't mean it, God, she whispered under her breath. If I cross my fingers he'll see and be angry, but I don't really mean it. OK?

'So now that we've got that world-shaking decision in hand, how about if we all go out and watch the great fisherman from Boston show us how to catch fish in a lake that doesn't have any?'

'I think I'd better stay ashore,' Mickey chuckled. 'It's too confining in that boat, and I'm afraid I might say something and he might hit me.'

'Hit you, dear?' The old man was altogether too solemn. 'Has he ever hit you?'

'No, Papa Gregory.' She took his arm, and was reminded again that the fine figure of a man had now become a bag of bones. 'No,' she repeated,' but it wasn't from lack of trying.' With which, being a firm believer in cowardice, she jumped back out of Harry's range.

The two men stood there for a moment, smiling and then turned toward the dock. But there had to be at least one more word. 'Do a good job, Harry,' she called after them. 'I'll get some vegetables together, and I'll cook what you catch for supper!'

Her loving brother, from behind his father's back, made an indecent gesture. She stood on the top step of the veranda and watched as they puttered out into the lake. When she went back into the house she went straight to her piano. Her fingers wandered through some of her old favourites while her mind wrestled with her problems.

There was a great deal of ground to be covered. Harry, first of all. Letting him run loose in the county would eventually throw him into the arms of Veronica Armstead. So Harry must be nailed down, and Sue Ellen was still the best nail.

Then George. Good lord, she had last seen him, the gash in his head still wet with blood, as his cousin loaded him into their car and previous afternoon. How could he have escaped her mind for so long? Now that Papa wanted to meet him, George would just have to move centre stage.

Despite her avowed priorities it was Sue Ellen she called first. The Alabama girl was very direct about the whole affair. Brother Harry was a fine man, but a barbarian, and not safe for a poor southern girl to be alone with. It took about half an hour of argument before Sue Ellen came round to a very timid 'perhaps'.

'And it will just be a simple dinner,' Mickey promised. 'No going outdoors—well, perhaps out to the veranda if you play your cards right. And early. Six o'clock, because Papa must eat then, right?'

Sue Ellen was still protesting about 'not wanting to play any cards at *all*' when Mickey hung up the telephone.

The call to George required a great deal more patience. George had a bad cold, a bad temper, and four stitches in his forehead. 'And you didn't give a damn,' he roared. 'I thought we were engaged!'

'But we are,' she returned desperately. 'We are. And George, there's something important——'

'Then make it short.' He punctuated his bad humour with a double sneeze that shook the whole telephone system. She shook her head, discouraged. But it's all your own fault, she told herself. Dear George was just trying to help out, and he got caught up in another one of your clumsy schemes! She made a few soothing sounds down the wire.

'The big news is that Papa has agreed to see you, George!' she told him, interrupting his diatribe. They were magic words. Her betrothed stopped in the middle of a sentence and coughed a time or two.

'You mean that—that he's going to approve our wedding?' The ill temper had disappeared. He was back to the lovable boyish George who had first attracted her. She chose her words carefully.

'He—George, I think he approves our engagement. I don't know about the wedding. He says he wants to get to know you. Isn't that important? Harry talked him into it. I was surprised at that!'

'Your brother?' She could almost see the hackles rise at the back of her finance's neck. 'Mickey, I know you think a great deal of your brother, but I must tell you I'm suspicious of him. Never trust a lawyer, that's what my father used to say.'

'Well, I'm sure we can trust Harry,' she protested. 'I've known him for ever so long; he's a man of his word. But that's not what I wanted to talk about, love. I thought—if you are feeling better—that tomorrow would be a good time to start. A family dinner, here at home? You and I, Papa, Harry—and I thought to invite Sue Ellen.'

'That little vamp?'

'It's something I have to do—for Harry,' she said in a very subdued tone.' I have this project that I have to take care of for Harry.'

'Not tomorrow,' he grumbled. 'I can't breathe through my nose. Make it the weekend?'

'I,—I hate to put it off,' she sighed. 'Well—all right. Saturday night? Promise?'

'All right,' he managed between coughs. 'Six o'clock, I suppose?'

'Yes, dear. For Papa's sake. You'll come?'

'Of course I'll come.'

'I love you, George.' She made a kissing sound.

'Of course you do,' he returned, and hung up.

She wandered back out into the kitchen, half in a dream. There was no more handsome man than George in all the world. If he's the man in my dreams, and he *has* to be, what a wild marriage we're going to have! Strange, though, he's never said he loved me. But of course he must. Men don't propose to girls if they don't love them. Re-word that—men don't propose *marriage* to girls——Her eyes flared open as she examined the kitchen.

'Darn that man!' she snapped. 'Look at all those dirty dishes. 'Oh, I'll help you with the dishes, Mickey'—isn't that what that scoundrel said? Unless something else comes up! Bah! I'll get even with you, Harry Butterworth!'

The 'getting even' scheme popped into her head about half an hour later, just as she looked through the kitchen window and saw the power-boat come slowly up to the dock. The two men climbed out, Harry offering his father an arm. Each carried a fishing rod. There was some joke being bandied about; they were both laughing. But outside of the fishing rod, they carried nothing.

Mickey put her mind into high gear, and her hands flew as she laid out the dinner. By the time the men had slowly climbed up to the house she had washed her hands, given her hair a quick pat or two, and met them at the door.

'Would you believe it? We didn't catch a thing,' Papa Gregory announced, with wry humour.

'Not even a minnow?' She stood in front of Harry, a broad smile on her face, her hands clasped behind her back, teasing.

'Not even a minnow,' he returned. 'And don't start gloating now.'

'Who, me?'

'You, Miss Innocence. Butter wouldn't melt on your nose!'

'In your mouth,' she corrected absent-mindedly. 'Don't you ever get any clichés right? And what do we do for dinner tonight? I was counting on some fine trout.'

'Well, too bad,' he muttered. 'I need a shower.'

Papa put an arm around her shoulder as they both watched Harry stomp off up the stairs.

'He didn't even put his fishing rod away,' she giggled.

'Watch your step, young lady,' her stepfather warned. 'A

nasty temper, that brother of yours has. You can only push him so far, you know.'

'I know,' she chuckled, not quite contritely. 'You'd better get a shower, too, Papa, and then take a little rest. Dinner will be in another—oh—half-hour?'

The older man gave her a squeeze, and kissed her cheek. 'You're a good girl, Mickey,' he said, and walked slowly off to clean up. She watched him, concerned, as he held on to the rail to help himself upstairs.

'No I'm not,' she muttered under her breath as she made for the kitchen. 'I am a mean, suspicious, arrogant woman who means to get even with Harry!'

The two men were back downstairs at six, Harry nursing a Scotch on the rocks, Papa Gregory making do with a glass of milk—and not appreciating it one bit. She gave them both a smile as she went past the living-room door on her way to set the table in the dining-room. 'Pretty soon?' Harry called, walking over to the door. 'I could eat an old shoe.'

'What a delightful idea,' she laughed, making a little face at him. 'I'll just have to poke around the kitchen and see if I can find one.'

He swung a hand at her as she went by, but long experience gave her the extra step that protected her backside from assault. She looked over her shoulder as she stood at the kitchen door. 'I told you you were getting along in years,' she mocked, and ducked into her workroom. It was nice, having the last word. She hummed as she bustled, happy at the way the day had ended. Or would soon end.

Both men came to the table when she rang the little dinner bell that hung outside the kitchen door. She helped Papa into his chair. 'You overdid it again,' she murmured in his ear as he pulled his chair up. 'You were supposed to take it easy, darn you!'

'Nag, nag, nag,' her stepfather chuckled. 'I need to marry you off in the worst way.'

'And that's the way it'll be,' Harry commented. 'In the worst way, I mean.'

'Oh, shut up and eat your meal,' Mickey snapped, hovering over Gregory's shoulder to be sure his steak was well done, his vegetables crisp.

'I would if I had something to eat,' Harry growled. She looked across the table at him. His face was grim, but his eyes were sparkling, as if daring her. It was all she needed. She walked around, picking up a covered dish from the serving table as she went by.

'I made something special for you,' she giggled, putting the plate in front of him. He looked up at her suspiciously.

'What are you up to?'

'Nothing,' she said, trying to look innocent. 'I really thought you were going to bring a fish or two back for dinner, so my plans just didn't work out. Luckily you reminded me of something. Eat. Eat in good health.'

His hand moved slowly to the knob on the cover. 'I'm just not sure I want to see this,' he said. 'All of a sudden I don't seem to be hungry.'

'Eat while it's warm,' his father directed. 'This is really tender steak, Mickey. She's got a good shopping eye, too, son. That's half the problem with concocting a good meal. What's that you——'

Harry had finally worked up his nerve. He lifted the cover off the dish. 'Why you little——' he roared, and started up from his chair.

'I couldn't find an old shoe,' Mickey laughed, dodging behind Papa's chair for protection. The two tiny sardines lay nose to nose in the middle of Harry's plate, glaring at him.

'I'll old shoe you,' he roared, coming around the table. Papa Gregory was laughing too hard to be any protection, she could see. She waited until Harry had committed himself, then raced down the other side of the table as fast as her legs could carry her. She slammed the dining-room door shut behind her, but dared not stop to turn the key that hung in the lock. The stairs were no obstacle. Mickey took them two at a time, losing one of her shoes in the doing. She could hear him close behind her as she scooted down the hall, dived into her room, and slammed the door behind her. Her hand fumbled for the key and managed to turn it before Harry's heavy fists thundered on the wood.

Laughter sent her into spasms. So much laughter that tears formed and ran down her cheeks.

'You'd better let me in,' he roared from outside in the hall.

'Sure I will,' she called back to him. 'On some February thirtieth. And not a day sooner, you hear? You don't fool me with that sweet talk, Harry Butterworth.'

'I'll tear you limb from limb,' he roared.

'Lover's talk,' she yelled back. 'Tell me some more!'

Ordinarily the discussion would have gone on for another ten minutes or so. Not this time. There was silence from outside her door, and yet she hadn't heard his footsteps retreating. She bit her lip, wondering. It's a trap; of course it is, she told herself. But she wasn't sure. And leaving Papa down there at the table, all alone, that was a problem. What was Harry up to?

She put her ear to the door. The hall clock was ticking away. The curtain at her window was rattling. You would think I could hear his heart if he were really there, she thought. Nothing.

Cautiously she turned the key, barely a centimetre at a time. When the lock clicked it sounded like a cannon going off. She laid an ear on the door panel again. Nothing from beyond it. Not a sound. Just as slowly her hand palmed the knob, and turned it gently. The door was old, the knob older. There was one spot in the centre of its turn where it squeaked. She jumped, then recovered her cool. Gently she drew the door inward and peered around its edge in both directions.

It was evening-dark in the upstairs hall; nobody had thought to turn on a light. But it seemed to be empty. Her smile crinkled her face as she stepped out cautiously, paused a second, and started on tiptoe for the stairs. Her hand was actually on the newel post when Harry's hand came down on top of hers.

'Oh, my God, you scared me!' Mickey half-screamed as she whirled around.

'I'll do more than that,' he snarled. She watched both his hands warily. He was too close for her to dodge him, but if he swung she might be able to duck under. It was not his intention. Instead of swinging, his arms closed around her, pulling her back up off the stair into the darkness.

'Do you know what happens to smart little girls who tease just once too often?' he murmured into her ear.

She was paralysed, caught in some emotional trap she could not explain. Her lips were dry. She ran her tongue around them. 'No,' she gasped. 'What?'

He pulled her hard against him, crushing her against his steel chest. Before she could close her mouth Harry's lips came down on hers, sealing her into a world that suddenly had become fire and cyclone.

That night she had the dream again, wilder and more wicked than ever before.

CHAPTER FIVE

RAIN shrouded the mountains, beat down the waves on the lake, and dripped from the bright summer leaves. A fitting end for a wild week, Mickey thought as she sat alone in the music room. The very name was a delusion, attached by her mother to the space that had once been a glass-enclosed greenhouse filled with flowers. Now everything was gone, leaving a bare expanse, well lit by a curved glass roof. And in the middle of it all sat her piano.

It was like playing outdoors in the rain, except that the drops only threatened, never landed. When she was a little girl it had seemed like a vast empty stadium, where old Mr Pelchoir came twice a week and drilled her, under her mother's watchful eye.

Mr Pelchoir, her mother and, in fact, the old piano were only ghosts now, spirits that she could see occasionally out of the far corners of her eyes. The replacement piano was a Baldwin Grand, a gift from Papa Gregory on her sixteenth birthday. It had marked two occasions. The first, a grand demonstration of her stepfather's love; the second, the day when she—and Papa Gregory—had sadly admitted that she had not the talent nor the concentration to be a successful concert pianist. That dream was long behind her, but the piano was still the instrument she came to when puzzled by life. As now.

Her fingers stabbed at the keys, fumbling her way

through a Chopin *étude*. The hands were moving automatically; her mind was on other things. The dinner party with Sue Ellen as the principal guest had proved to be a total flop. The girl, outwardly sophisticated, had gone shy in Harry's presence. Perhaps it had something to do with the snake incident and her embarrassment. Or perhaps she was just overwhelmed by Harry.

Mickey's fingers wandered, almost playing the notes that Chopin had written. Overwhelmed by Harry. What a strange thought. When you came right down to it, he wasn't even handsome. Oh, good to look at, in a strong masculine way, but certainly not handsome. His eyebrows were far too heavy, and there seemed to be nothing he could do to regulate his thick brown hair. On top of which he was undoubtedly the most arrogant, domineering pain in the neck who had ever put on long trousers! That was the trouble with these Butterworth men. Papa Gregory had it, too. When he put his foot down, even the ocean shook. Now how in the world did a sweet, quiet person like my mother handle a man like that? she wondered.

A smile toyed at the corners of her mouth. Now *there* was a project worthy of research. Deny it if you will, Mickey, but no matter how many feet were put down, how many masculine voices were raised in rage, when Mama dug in her heels things always ended up being done her way. I need to think about that, Mickey told herself. How did she do it?

'That's plagiarism,' the deep voice behind her said. Mickey jerked her hands back from the keyboard and whirled around.

'You——' she sputtered.

'As you say—me,' Harry laughed. 'Caught you by

surprise, did I? That song you're making up is almost all Chopin. He wouldn't be pleased. I don't remember if there's something about it in the copyright laws.'

'I wasn't making it up,' she said, dropping her hands into her lap. 'And he's been dead a long time. What have you come to devil me about today?'

'What's this? No bright "Good morning, brother"? Come to think of it I haven't laid an eye on you for two days.' He came around to her side and lounged against the lid of the piano. 'Can it be you've been avoiding me?'

'Probably,' she muttered. 'Don't you think you deserve it for that—demonstration—Wednesday night?'

'Demonstration? You mean my efforts to be a congenial host to your friend Sue.'

'Sue Ellen. She hates to be called Sue. Nobody says that in Alabama.'

'Ah, yes, Sue Ellen. I must remember that— in case I ever run into her again.'

'Oh, lord, Harry,' Mickey moaned. 'I'm just trying to help, that's all. Sue Ellen would make you a wonderful wife. And I know your tastes better than you do.'

'Do you really?'

'Yes I do,' she continued stubbornly. 'If I leave it all to you, you'll end up with somebody like Veronica Armstead. That girl's the pits. The absolute bottom-level pits!'

'Strange that I hadn't noticed that,' he returned solemnly. 'And here I've gone to a lot of trouble to invite her over for dinner tomorrow night.'

'Oh, no! No, you can't do that, Harry. Give her a ring. Make it some other night. Not tomorrow!'

'Dear God, is it all that much trouble, one guest for an ordinary Saturday night dinner? I could go out and get pizza if that's the case.'

'It's not that.' She swivelled around to face him, putting one of her long-fingered hands on his wrist. 'I've already invited George to come tomorrow night—he's been ill—and I thought tomorrow night would be just the time for him to talk to Papa, and——'

'Oh, now it comes clear. You think my manners might upset the wagon? I swear I'll be on my best behaviour. Cross my heart.' He proceeded to do just that, making the motions across his white sweater—the one she had made for him the year before.

She pushed herself back from the piano keyboard and stood up gracefully. 'It's not your manners I worry about, Harry, honestly. When you're not playing the clown you're as well-mannered as any man I know. You actually scared Sue Ellen, did you know that?'

'Scared her? Just because I hustled her out here to dance? If you hadn't been so reluctant about playing there wouldn't have been a cross word spoken all evening!'

'So now it's my fault?' Her eyes fired up, and the blaze spilled over and out. 'Now it's my fault you dragged her out here like some harem slave, and demanded—commanded—that I play. Two hours, non-stop. Who the devil do you think I am, anyway? My wrists were so sore that night I couldn't sleep a wink. And you whirling Sue Ellen around like some darned puppet. For goodness' sake, Harry, no matter what I played you insisted on waltzing. And you didn't even have the decency to take her home afterwards!'

'Now why should I do that?' he purred. 'She had you to drive her. Did she really need me?'

Mickey's shoulders slumped. 'I guess not,' she muttered.

'She was so out of breath she couldn't say a word. Until she got to her house, that is.'

He chuckled. 'I'm waiting with bated breath for that word. What did she say?'

'She's my best friend in Miller's Gap. She said *goodbye.*'

'That's a nice short line, not too difficult for her memory, I suppose. Goodbye until you scheme up something else?'

'Goodbye, period. She drove down to Albany that same night, and took the first plane back to Alabama. You're mean, Harry Butterworth. Just plain mean.'

A one-sided smile played at his mouth as he dropped down on the piano stool and played an experimental note or two. 'You're a great musician, too,' she noted bitterly.

'Hey, I'm a lawyer,' he returned. There was a whisper of contrition in his voice. 'I had no time to study music. Did it really hurt—my running off your best friend?'

'Well it didn't feel good, if that's what you mean. I don't have a lot of friends, that I could afford to throw one away.'

'Would it help if I said I'm sorry?'

'Of course not. I know you too well, Harry Butterworth. You could *say* sorry as glibly as you want, but you'd never *mean* sorry.'

One of his hands trapped her wrist, gently. 'Well, I really *am* sorry,' he said softly. 'You may not know it, but your happiness means a lot to me.'

'I can see it does,' she snapped, pulling away from him. 'Making fun of my friends, doing—things—to me in the hall, always teasing at me. Yes, I can see how much my happiness means to you. When I was in school we used to say, it ain't what you say do that counts, but what you do do.'

He essayed a few more notes on the piano. She stood

straight and strong—and shivering—beside him. Most of
her relationships with her brother had been roller-coaster:
up one minute, down the next. But now there was a gloom,
a dread that held her, shook her confidence in her little
world. She felt like a little chick, pecking around inside her
eggshell, and then suddenly bursting through to find that
things were so entirely different outside. An outside where
brothers hurt cruelly, friends disappeared, and real enemies
existed. She felt like running off to cry, but her legs would
not move.

'You know,' Harry mused, his head down over the
keyboard, 'I spent some time in Miller's Gap yesterday.'
He paused. She stubbornly refused to comment.

'I had a few beers down at the tavern, bowled a couple of
lines at the alley—like that. You'd be surprised at the old
story going the rounds again in the village.'

'Would I?' She wanted it to sound cold, uninterested.
Instead it came out as a rusty squeak. He looked up quickly
and then turned away and hit another note or two.

'You would. Somebody's been resurrecting history
around these parts. Everyone I met wanted to tell me about
the Devlin fortune.'

'Oh, no, Harry!' Her face flushed. He had got her
attention in a hurry. 'Not that old fantasy. Not after all
these years.'

'Yeah, that old turkey. Would you believe it, somebody
has actually been asking around town, digging up all the
details. About how your grandfather was the richest man in
the north counties, and owned half the land from Albany to
the state line.'

'Oh, God! It's not true!'

'There are people who believe it, Mickey. Your grandfather was the biggest conman in western New York. He could have sold the Brooklyn Bridge if he hadn't been busy selling shares in Niagara Falls.'

'Don't, please, Harry. I never knew him, but my mother loved him very much. He couldn't have been all bad.'

'I know that,' he laughed. 'He was a wily old soul, and I don't condemn him for it. But the rumours still hang on. And what I hear is that some writer is going to do a book about him, and has been asking questions everywhere.'

'Questions? What kind of questions?'

'Like, who inherits all the old man's fortune.'

'That's silly. My mother did, what there was of it. It really wasn't much. You know that.'

'Ah, but you see, nobody else does, Mickey.'

'I—I don't understand any of this,' she sighed. 'Or even why you brought it up. I think I'd better get back to the housework.'

'And that's another thing,' he said sharply, standing up as he closed the lid over the keyboard. 'I don't see why you have to run around this place with a broom in your hand when we could afford to hire a dozen people to do so.'

'There's a lot you don't see, Harry. Like, we're a long way from the big city lights, and there aren't many people in the area who want to be taken on as domestics, or——What the devil do you care? I'm the housekeeper. That's what I do for a living. You're the lawyer; why don't you just go about your lawyering and keep your nose out of my housekeeping?' She stormed away from him, the set of her back telling what her voice would not.

He caught up with her at the double doors that shut the music room off from the rest of the house. One of his hands came over her head and pushed against the door she was trying to pull open. She stamped her foot in anger, the blood boiling up to her cheeks.

'So it's OK if I bring my girlfriend to supper?'

'I don't care,' she snarled. 'Bring a dozen of them. Have an orgy!'

'Sounds good,' he chuckled, as he released the pressure and let her open the door. She scuttled through and dived for the kitchen. It was a place which neither of the men invaded. My domain, she told herself angrily. Woman's place is in the kitchen!

If I had any sense at all, she thought as she banged around needlessly among the pots and pans, I wouldn't lift another finger to help him. I'd let him fall into that witch's trap and get himself scalded for life. He doesn't deserve the help of a very nice person like myself! Which, on second thoughts, was funny enough to drive away the anger and bring a chuckle to her lips.

The rain let up at six o'clock that night, and as the clouds dispersed to eastwards Mickey's temper improved as well. There was planning to be done if the next day's dinner was to be the success she wanted it to be. George . . . If she wanted him to be a winner, he had to be packaged and presented in the way that Papa Gregory expected. She phoned him on Saturday morning and arranged to meet him in town for a preparatory session. McGregor's Malt Shop was the place.

Nobody in town remembered who McGregor might have been, but his shop had been serving malts and coffee and cakes for more years than the Pavilion had been standing. There was a small table squeezed into the very back corner, with a bench seat and a window. She was there at nine o'clock. George arrived at nine-thirty.

Mickey was up and around the table before he was half-way across the room, almost upsetting her coffee cup in the process. 'Oh, George!' His Greek beauty was marred by a very artfully placed plaster just above the right eyebrow. He was dressed, as always, in the best of casual wear. His light blond hair was just slightly disarranged, drooping down over his forehead to conceal the blue and green bruise. He moved stiffly, like the battered but victorious gladiator. She just could not hold back. Despite his repeated admonitions, she threw her arms around his neck and stretched up to peck at his cheek.

'Not here, Michele,' he muttered. 'Everyone is watching.'

'Who cares?' she giggled. 'Look.' She held up her hand and displayed her engagement ring. 'I've been wearing it night and day, George!' Her hand looped over his arm as she led him back to the table. He required a great deal of settling. His neck bothered him, he said.

'Not so bad that you can't come tonight?' she asked anxiously.

'Oh, no. Not that bad.' He gave her one of his patented Spartan looks: with your shield or on it—that sort of thing. It was perhaps just a little corny, but Mickey had learned to put up with it over the past two months. Put up with it, she thought? Revel in it. So why am I being so—so picky today? Dear George.

She ordered for them both. More coffee and a bagel for herself, a full breakfast for George. It was habit more than anything else, and it pleased her to be useful to somebody. Papa Gregory at home; George here. He seemed to blossom under the attention. When he appeared to be at the proper summit, she began to lay it out.

'Now George, tonight you have to be an actor. Papa especially likes——' And so forth, for twenty-five minutes. He was a quick student; he could have been an actor, she told herself. But then he had ambitions. His book—and now this real estate thing. More irons in the fire than any man she had ever known. Well, perhaps not as many as Harry.

She was half-way through her little schemer-script when George interrupted. 'That house,' he asked. 'Does your father own the house?'

'Stepfather,' she corrected, and then giggled. 'Oh, no. Didn't you know? The house is part of the Devlin fortune. The house and six acres of land around it.'

'You must tell me about the Devlin fortune,' he mused. 'I keep hearing the word all over town.'

'Not now, George, please. It's——' She was about to say, it's just a funny story, when he interrupted again.

'That's your brother,' he said softly. 'Outside with my cousin. What do you suppose they're up to?'

'Beats me,' she said quickly, 'but whatever it is, he's up to no good.'

'You're probably right,' her fiancé said. 'Look, I don't feel like talking to your brother. I think I'll just slip out the back way.'

'But you have to come tonight,' she wailed.

'He'll be there?'

'Yes, of course. He's bringing your cousin to dinner. But you have to be there, George. We hardly seem to spend any time at all together lately.'

He patted her hand. 'That won't be for long. When's your birthday?'

'Next month. The tenth. Three weeks from today.'

'Mark it down on your calendar,' he chuckled. 'That will

be the day.'

'For what,' she asked suspiciously.

'For our wedding,' he announced grandly. He seemed to have recovered all his suppleness as he slid out from behind the table, squeezed her hand, and headed for the back door. She smiled after him, and kept on smiling until Maizy Gordon came with the bill.

'You payin' again, Mickey?'

'Of course,' she said, coming out of her little daze. 'George isn't established yet.'

'Yeah,' the elderly waitress said. 'I've noticed. Have a good day.'

Outside the door Mickey tried her best to duck out of sight, but was not fast enough. Harry dragged Veronica back and yelled at Mickey until she could not ignore him. She turned around, trying to look startled.

'I didn't see you, Harry. Good morning.' The greeting was addressed to Veronica, and was somewhat less than warm. I just can't like that woman, Mickey told herself. She's no good for Harry, and just the sort who will latch on to him like a leech!

'I was telling Veronica how you were going to serve us something special tonight,' he went on blandly. 'I don't think people around these parts know what a capable chef you are.' He beamed at them both, as if he were a missionary explaining gourmet cuisine to cannibals.

'Mickey hardly gets around,' Veronica contributed. 'Nobody knows much about her at all. She's the shy type—except with George, of course. You have no idea, Harry, how many times I've had to avoid coming home, to give the lovebirds time to bill and coo!' Her little trill of laughter ran upscale.

B flat, Mickey thought, when it should have been a natural. And what is she up to now? I've never been in or outside George's house. Never. But why should I tell Harry that? Look at his face. He looks just like the boy who bit into the sour apple!

'I'm not a chef, I'm a cook,' she said, deciding to shift ground. 'And it will certainly be a surprising meal.' She smiled sweetly at Veronica. It certainly would be a surprise. Here it was, ten o'clock in the morning, and she hadn't decided what to serve yet. Another can of sardines?

'And of course you won't tell us what you're planning?' He had re-grouped, and was smiling again. Isn't that silly, she told herself. I don't understand my own brother. He blows hot and cold so often I think he must have a switch someplace that just automatically changes back and forth!

Veronica saved her the trouble of thinking up some lie. 'We are looking for a place that serves a second breakfast,' the other woman interjected. 'Do you recommend this one?' Veronica's nose wrinkled, as if she expected a negative answer.

'Well, it's dark and narrow and local,' Mickey commented in her best manner. 'But it has two advantages. They keep it very clean, and it's the only one in town. You must excuse me.' She offered them both a polite smile, and made off down the street.

She heard Harry chuckle as she walked away, but Veronica said 'Well!' in a very condescending voice. Well indeed, Mickey thought as she ducked into the supermarket. 'Very well. Score one more for the home team.'

The few customers clustered around the bread rack next to her gave her a curious look. She shrugged her shoulders, lifted both hands in an apologetic manner, and started planning. Something unusual. The market had only one unusual item on hand: frozen rock Cornish hen. She bought enough for eight, allowing for drop-ins and accidents. Mr Bronson, who had been trying to unload that item for three weeks, gave her a big smile at the cash register. The smile, of course, was hardly as big as the bill.

She hurried home, taking time to track down Papa Gregory and wish him good morning. 'You ate your cereal? And the fruit?'

'I ate,' he returned. 'If you can call that a breakfast.'

She soothed him with the promise of a sumptuous dinner, and then went back into the kitchen to lay on the meal.

There was more work involved than she had expected. The birds had thawed by one in the afternoon, but the problem of stuffing them with her own variation of wild rice, mushrooms and bacon was not easily solved. Papa Gregory grumbled. His light breakfast had been followed by an even lighter lunch. Thank God Harry had not come home.

She thought all that as she collapsed in the old kitchen rocking chair at about two-thirty. The room looked like the location of the last earthquake, with dirty pots and pans scattered around, half-prepared dishes still waiting for her attention, and the oven heating up for action on a day when the outside temperature had already passed eighty degrees and was heading for a new record.

You have three alternatives, she told herself wearily. Throw everything out and start again on roast-beef sandwiches. Or pack a bag and run off before anyone notices. Or just sit there and let them all starve to death. As usual, with a fertile mind, she chose the fourth. She inserted the stuffed fowl, checked the oven temperature, splashed water on her flushed face, and went out the back door into the flower garden which her grandmother had started, and Mickey had continued. There was peace to be found among the flowers. Peace, and a little touch of cool wind off the lake.

Her garden was a mixture of values. The last of the tulips were blooming. Scarlet and gold and dark blue, they hung their heads next to the asters, not yet in flower, but promising. Over in one corner there was still a bunch of violets, long past their time, but trying. And over it all the scent of woodlands. Mile after mile of mountains and dales, stretching north to the Canadian border in the Adirondack Park, a mixed land of wild and settled areas, all under environmental control to regulate further development. She picked one of the blooms from the violet patch. Its five blue petals fanned out bravely from a white centre and yellow core. She buried the tip of her stubby nose in its fragrance, and felt renewed.

Things went more smoothly for the remainder of the afternoon. The birds were browning nicely in the oven. Asparagus tips and small glazed carrots were the vegetables. But it was five o'clock before she came that far, and dessert was yet to be made. Her courage failed her. There was a package-mix for chocolate mousse, made with a non-sugar sweetener. She whipped it up quickly, shoved it in the refrigerator, and hurried upstairs to bathe and dress.

The house seemed to be coming to life as she lay in the bath, soaking. She might have lain there for hours, barely floating at the level of the bath bubbles, had not Harry appeared on the scene. He tried the knob. Luckily she had remembered, and turned the key. His fist bounced off the door panel.

'Come on, woman! Dear God, you don't have all that much to wash. Get a-moving, girl. I have to shave and shower, too, you know.'

Not all that much to wash? She sat up, water cascading. Well, maybe he was right. She hadn't a great deal of flesh on her bones, but what she had was nicely packed. Not up to Sue Ellen's pulchritude, by any means, but—a nice handful, George had said. She wasn't sure exactly what he meant, but it had sounded like a compliment, and she meant to take it that way.

'Huh! A lot you know, Harry Butterworth,' she yelled through the door. 'I'll come when I'm ready!' His heavy fist banged twice more. The door trembled in its frame, and Mickey had a sudden change of mind.

'All right,' she yelled, 'I'm ready. Honest. I'm ready!' She scrambled up, spilling water out on the rug. The fist banged again. 'I'm coming!' A big bath towel was hurriedly transformed into a sarong. The water was gurgling down the drain. No time for her hair, for admiration; the darned bear was at the door. She flicked the lock.

He stood back to let her pass. 'Like a wet rat,' he muttered. 'And what a mess. Is that the way your mother taught you to leave a bathroom?'

'No,' she grumbled, 'I learned that from my brother!'

'Don't count on my good behaviour,' he yelled after her as she fled down the hall. 'I could turn mean.'

'So what else is new?' she muttered, slamming her bedroom door behind her and dropping exhaustedly on to her bed. It took about three minutes for the grin to reach her lips. It had always been this way between her and Harry. Papa Gregory had objected at first, but Mama had told him to ignore it. 'Love words,' she would say when they got too noisy. 'They think a lot of each other.' And we do, Mickey assured herself as she strugled to her feet and dried off. It takes a lot of loving to be able to live with a man like Harry for all these years. Or vice versa. With a giggle she started on the tedious brushing of all that bright red hair. Maybe I'll have it cut, she thought.

After George and I get married. I wouldn't dare to now—Harry would go right through the roof!

Dressing was not a problem. The whole purpose of the evening was to impress Papa, which meant a demure dress with a high neck, lace collar, short sleeves, a knee-length skirt. It was in a very pale shade of yellow, to set off her hair. It would not be a formal evening, just—dignified. Mickey wove her hair into one loose braid, and brought if forward to hang in front, over her left shoulder. Flat shoes. She wuld have liked to wear heels, but as well as looking nice she had to do all the serving. Three-inch spikes were definitely out.

A touch of her favourite perfume, and—no, that wasn't right, either. She had never bought a bottle of perfume in her whole life, although she always had plenty. Harry bought it. From her youngest days, when she had been eight and he sixteen, Harry had selected her perfume, bought it with his own money, and left it on her dressing-table without comment. It had only been in the last year or two that she had realised that not all brothers were as nice.

She could hear the two men getting ready as she went downstairs. Back in her apron, she poked at the birds, checked the mousse, and set up the individual servings of shrimp cocktail, then out to set the table. The best of everything. The Noritake bone china, the sterling silverware, candles for the two candelabra. Everything was ready. She went back into the kitchen again, set the dinner up on hotplates on her wheeled serving trolley, and took off the apron.

Her two men were talking out in the living-room. She could hear snatches as their identical baritones rose and fell. Law, stock market, terrorism. It was like hearing a homily. When the doorbell rang she took a step or two towards the front, then changed her mind and dropped back into the rocking-chair.

Harry went to welcome the guests.

Ten minutes later, composed but flushed, Mickey came out to join the others. They were sitting in the comfortable old armchairs in the living-room. Harry was up first, George a hesitant moment later. Papa claimed the rights of patriarchy and stayed in his chair, smiling.

'Doesn't my Michele look a sight to see?' Gregory commented. 'You'd never know that she's been working all afternoon.' Harry cocked an eyebrow at her and grinned. Mickey nodded to Veronica and walked across the room to George, accepting his hug, and kissing him on the cheek. The men sat down again and picked up the conversation. Mickey perched herself on the arm of George's chair, her hand resting lightly on his shoulder.

'The trouble with all this,' George said, 'is that we all could make millions by developing the land around here, but the law prohibits it. Millions!'

'And lose the only wilderness area left to the state,' Harry commented. 'For millions of people this park is all there is left of the American wilderness.'

George was not to be deterrred. 'Look at this house,' he said. 'This whole area could be converted to fifteen flats with a minimum amount of work. You're sitting on a goldmine, Judge Butterworth.'

'Not me,' Papa Gregory chuckled. 'Mickey. The house, the land, it all belongs to the Devlins. And Mickey is the last of the Devlins.'

George leaned forward, his nose twitching. 'You mean all this? Everything?'

'That's just what I mean,' Papa Gregory returned. 'Her mama's will left all the Devlin fortune to Mickey. Of course, there are some stipulations.'

'Stop it,' Mickey giggled. Surely they all knew it was a joke? This house and land, yes. Beyond that the famous Devlin fortune consisted of one sterling-silver punch ladle, reputed to have been made by Paul Revere himself, and a salt-cellar which might or might not be silver. It was so encrusted that it was black. Ornately formed, but black. The Devlin fortune—huh!

'Mickey's embarrassed to be found out. She's a real live heiress,' Harry added solemnly. 'Of course, the word is out all over this part of the state. I'm sure you've heard it before, Armstead?'

'Well, it's hard not to hear something about it,' George responded. 'Still, you never know the details, you know. What did you mean, stipulations?'

Veronica took that moment to interrupt. 'I wish I had a drink,' she suggested. 'I find all this excitement makes me dry.'

Mickey jumped to her feet. 'I—I'm sorry,' she stuttered. 'I just wasn't thinking. What would you prefer?'

'I'll get it.' Harry stood up and ambled over to the hand-carved mahogany cupboard where the drinks were stored.

'I'll bring some ice,' Mickey murmured, and rushed out to the kitchen to do so. By the time she returned George and Veronica had been served. Something and vodka, it looked to be. Harry relieved her of the ice-bucket and passed a piece to each of them with the tongs. Still murmuring excuses, red-faced, Mickey rushed back to the kitchen for the iced tea which was all Papa Gregory could have, and all *she* ever wanted. Harry was proposing a toast when she came back.

'To the Devlin fortune,' he said, and lifted his glass. George turned to touch glasses with Mickey as she returned to his side. 'To us,' he whispered. She smiled back at him, still under some strain of embarrassment.

'But you never did say about the stipulations,' Veronica prompted. She was tapping her glass with one long fire-red fingernail.

'Simple enough,' Papa said, his voice cloaked in his judicial robes. 'Mickey inherits everything on her twenty-fifth birthday.'

'Twenty-fifth?' George looked up to her for confirmation.

'Yes, twenty-fifth,' Papa continued smoothly. He smiled down into his glass and took another sip. What an act, Mickey told herself. He hates iced tea. Look at him. You'd think it was the world's best brandy. And his son is giving us a show, too. What the devil are the pair of them up to? And no, I'm not being disloyal to my family. A girl who can't work up a good healthy suspicion of her brother has never had a brother like Harry!

'Oh, there is a provision,' Harry added idly. He was twirling his glass, staring into the mixture. Gregory was staring at George. 'If our Mickey were to get married, with the permission of her trustee, before she's twenty-five, but after her twenty-first birthday, why she gets the whole thing immediately.'

'I'm glad you brought that up,' George said. His cousin, sitting next to him, gave him a slight nudge with her shoe. He ignored it. 'I came with a purpose. You all might as well know that Mickey and I would like your permission, Judge, to be married on her birthday.'

'Is that so?' Papa Gregory was heaving himself to his feet, a broad smile on his face. 'A laudable ambition,' he agreed, 'but I'm afraid it has nothing to do with me. Harry is Mickey's trustee. Why don't you apply to him? And in the meantime, ladies, let's go in to supper.'

CHAPTER SIX

MICKEY came walking up from the tiny beach at four o'clock on Sunday afternoon, shrugged into her towelling robe for comfort. Lake swimming required a great deal of sunshine, and after the rains of Friday and Saturday the water was cold. But the exercise had worked out the kinks, in both her muscles and her brain, and made her feel better. Papa was taking his usual siesta, and Harry was swaying slightly on the porch swing, trying to imitate a newspaper reader.

It wasn't a very good imitation. His head was tilted against the back of the swing, mouth half open. A gurgling sound pulsed from his throat. A person who didn't know him would swear he was asleep. Someone who did know him might feel the same. Mickey walked barefoot over beside him and looked her fill. I'll speak to him today, she decided. He doesn't deserve it, but I'll be nice to him. She pulled off her bathing cap and let her hair fall down around her. Something must have alerted him. When next she looked down, one of those big brown eyes was fixed on her.

'Mickey?' It was a groggy salute. The other eye struggled open before she could answer.

'I'm being nice to you,' she announced firmly.

He sat up slowly, recognising the words for what they were—a declaration of war.

His feet came down on to the veranda floor. 'Being nice to

me? How nice.' The eyes had half closed again, warily. He conspicuously inspected both her hands for weapons. 'Why do I deserve all this niceness?'

'You don't deserve it,' she said. 'I'm doing it just because *I'm* basically a nice person.'

'And I'm not? Is that what I should deduce? What sort of a bathing suit is that you're wearing?'

She looked down. Her robe had come unfastened. She used the loose sides as a towel to dry herself off. He was only trying to change the subject, but she couldn't help answering anyway. 'It's my black costume,' she returned. 'I've had it for years.'

'I can see that,' he chuckled. 'There's a great deal more of you now than there was when you bought it.'

She stamped her foot in anger. 'Don't you make fun of me, Harry Butterworth. And don't try to change the subject. Sometimes I think you're not worth being nice to!'

'Probably not,' he agreed. 'All right, Mickey. Lay it on me. What have I done that's so terrible?'

'You ruined my dinner party, that's what you did! And I hated you for it. All last night I hated you. I hope you couldn't sleep a wink.'

'So that's what it was. Well, you had your wish. I couldn't sleep a wink all night long. And there I was blaming it on the stuffing in that bird!'

'There was nothing wrong with the stuffing, Harry, and you know it. How could you say such a thing?'

'I know,' he offered apologetically. 'Sit down here, Mickey. We'll talk it out.' He patted the cushion next to him in invitation. She sighed. Brothers were sometimes more trouble than they were worth. But then again——

'To clear the air, let me make a statement,' he said.

'There was absolutely nothing wrong with the meal. It was stupendous. From the shrimp cocktail to the chocolate mousse, there was nothing wrong with the meal. Perfect. You'll make some man a fine wife, my dear.'

'Not if you keep treating George the way you did at supper,' she snapped. 'How could you do that, Harry?'

'It wasn't hard,' he chuckled, and then choked down his enjoyment as her eyes glittered. 'Well—think about it. Did I really say anything so terrible? All I did was to get your young man talking. That's what Papa wanted, you know. To hear him expound.'

'Yes, you were a big help,' she muttered bitterly. 'You were egging him on like crazy. All that about developing properties up here, and getting the law changed. He didn't even know Papa is the president of the State Conservation League!'

'Is he really? I had forgotten.'

'One thing I know about you, Harry, is you never forget anything. Not the slightest thing. You knew. Admit it.'

'Well—perhaps I did. But that's what your George wanted to talk about, love. I only helped him out. And I thought his talk about acid rain was rather—quaint, too.'

'He's not a scientist,' she almost shouted, 'he's——'

'He's what? That would be nice to know. We spent three hours at the table and I couldn't find out just what he is.'

'He's an author.' She balled her hands to keep them from hitting him on their own. The nails were cut short, but still bit into her palms. 'He's an author. Some day he's going to be famous.'

'Oh? You've read the book?'

'Well—no. He doesn't want anybody to read it until its finished. But I know it'll be a wonder.' She shook her head. Drops were running down her neck from that segment of her hair she could not cram into her swimming cap. The spray hit him in the face.

'Hey, you don't have to drown me.'

'You deserve it. And then all that nonsense about the Devlin fortune. You know darn well it isn't worth—well, it isn't.'

'It's worth a little more than you think, Mike. True, the land can't be developed. But real estate prices are going up astronomically in this state. You could get a really good price for this place. At least up in the five-figure range.'

'That much? For such an old place as this?'

'You'd better believe it. And that salt-cellar. I've coveted that thing all my life. If we ever cleaned it up I'm sure it would prove to be a Cellini.' She turned sideways to look at him. His face was perfectly sober, but deep in his eyes humour gleamed.

'Oh, Harry, you're impossible! A Cellini? Stop pulling my leg.' All her anger disappeared. She huddled up close to him, tucking her hands under his arm, and resting her head on his shoulder.

'I take it this is a sign of forgiveness?'

She shook his arm the tiniest bit. 'You don't deserve it, but I forgive you,' she teased. 'I don't know about George.'

'I don't know about George either,' he sighed. 'What is it that you don't know?'

'I—I wish you wouldn't say that. I don't know if he'll ever forgive you. You made him sound like a fool. Even his cousin was kicking at his ankle under the table. I think she was trying to send him some message.'

'Doesn't it all give you pause to think?'

'I suppose it would if I had a great deal of money, but

I don't. George loves me because I'm me, and I love him the same way. There's no use trying to change my mind, Harry.'

'No, of course not,' he mused. 'That would be silly. But just suppose you had a great deal of money. Then what?'

'It's not likely to happen, so you can stop worrying,' she laughed. She squirmed around to bring her feet up on to the divan and get comfortable.

'Papa asked me to come out here for two reasons,' Harry continued, looking off into the distance. 'He wanted me to tell you about his operation, and he wanted me to make out his will.'

The swing rocked back and forth a few times under the prodding from his right foot. It took that long for the message to sink through.

'His will?'

'Now, don't go off into a cloud. He'll be with us for some time, Mickey. He just has this tendency to keep things orderly. Prior planning. Under his old will Mama was the beneficiary.'

'But Harry—I'm no lawyer, but I know you can't make out his will if you're the——'

'Beneficiary. It's a big word,' he laughed. 'And you're right.'

'Then I just don't understand,' she said wearily. 'I just don't understand.'

'So I'll explain. Lawyers are good at explaining. When I set up my own offices in Boston, Papa gave me my share of the inheritance. He said I would need it more then than later. Everything else goes to the daughter of the house.'

'But Harry, there isn't any daughter of the house.'

'Oh yes, there is, Mickey, and you is it!'

'No—Harry, he can't do that. I won't take it. I never did really get to be a Butterworth, you know. Papa said something about changing my name by deed poll, whatever that is, but Mama said I should decide for myself, and nothing happened.'

'You're too late to change the will, love. I brought a couple of people out from the village this afternoon as witnesses. It's all signed and sealed.'

'Harry, you don't know what you're doing to me,' she sighed. 'Papa has a deal of money, I suppose——'

'A very great deal,' he agreed.

'But can't you see, Harry? Darn you both! Now I'll be looking around corners, wondering if anybody likes me or is it just my money.' A tear formed at the corner of her eye. 'Damn you, Harry, it's all your doing, isn't it? You're just trying to make me suspicious of——Well, George will never know.'

'Not unless you tell him, Mickey.' She looked up into his face. The tone of his voice had changed. The corners of his mouth turned down, and his eyes had gone suddenly dull. He reached down and treasured one of her hands, scanned the lake for a moment, and then turned to her.

'I'm sorry, Mickey,' he said softly. 'I've been trying to do a number on you, and it's not right. As you said the other night, you have a right to chose your own form of happiness. I'm sorry. I'm a very arrogant, mean, dominating——'

'Brother,' she interrupted. 'And you're not really any of those things—well, not always.' She slid down the incline of the seat cushion again and tucked her head down on his shoulder.

'It's all so strange, though. I have this feeling that the

world is about to change completely, Harry, and I'm a little bit scared. I never did get to be a Butterworth, and now in a few weeks I won't even be a Devlin. Is it natural to be so scared?'

Harry cuddled her a little closer. 'I'm sure it is,' he comforted. 'I suppose it means a great deal more to a woman than to a man. Men don't have this identity problem. but keep your chin up, love. No matter what happens you'll always be a Butterworth—just as you always have been. You can hear the bells ringing to mark my words.'

'That's the telephone, you fool. Go and answer it. I'm catching my death of cold in this outfit.' She gave him a none too gentle push that almost knocked him over. He imitated a growl, and sent off smiling. She sat where she was for a moment, hugging herself. With just a few words he could comfort her. Wonderful things, relatives! The smile tugged at her lips as she sauntered upstairs, snatched up clothes for the evening, and went into the bathroom for a quick shower.

Mickey was back in her room, enveloped in an old robe, her newly washed hair done up in a towel, when Harry banged on her door and walked in.

'There's a part there where you're supposed to wait until I say "come in",' she told him as her fingers rubbed briskly at the ends of her hair.

'I knew there was something I'd forgotten,' he chuckled. 'Here, let me help you with that.'

She slipped out of the turban and leaned back as his strong sensitive fingers rubbed at her scalp. 'No hairdryer?'

'Bottom drawer,' she said dreamily. Another old habit,

coming back to haunt her. It was hard to remember how many times Harry had come in to help her dry her hair. It had been part of an old bargain. She had wanted short hair. Her mother had agreed; Harry held out against it. Mama had produced the compromise: Mickey would wear her hair long, but Harry would have to help out with the drying. She had been nine years old then. It was the sort of compromise where all sides had won. She loved it as he carefully worked behind her, and he claimed that he loved to do it. She leaned back to rest against his strength as he worked. It was over too soon.

While she fumbled for a tie to hold her hair back, he went over to her bed and sank back against the pillows. 'The call was from Dr Philbert,' he said. 'You know him?'

'He's the surgeon—one of the Friday night poker crew,' she returned. 'A short tubby little man. He wears a beard because nothing will grow on top of his head. At least that's what he said. Something wrong?' She turned around to stare at him, anxiety creeping up on her again. 'Harry?'

'No, not really wrong.' He smiled at her; it lit up his homely face, and made him quite—quite handsome, she thought.

'The good doctor says he has a cancellation for the day after tomorrow—for Papa's operation. He wants us to deliver him tomorrow morning for pre-op tests.'

'Get him down to Albany by tomorrow morning? We can't do that, Harry. He'd be all tired out—and then what would happen? It would mean leaving very early in the morning, before sunrise.'

'Ever hear of helicopters?'

'I—I never thought of that. Sometimes I think there's no end to my stupidities. Can you get one?'

'Already laid on,' he returned. 'It will be here half an hour after sunrise. Flight time is about one hoiur, give or take a few traffic problems. I think you'd better stay here.'

'No such thing!' She glared at him. 'If you think I'm going to stay up here while Papa is in hospital, you've got another think coming, Harry Butterworth!'

He sat up on the bed, laughing. 'I was thinking about lover-boy,' he returned. 'You don't really want to run off and leave him all alone up here, do you?'

'I don't have to worry about George,' she said stoutly. 'He'll understand. Now if you'll kindly absent yourself so I can get dressed, I'll see about supper.'

But all the while her hands were busy in the kitchen, her mind was not sure at all about George. So when the men went out on the veranda she sneaked a telephone call to her fiancé.

'He isn't in,' Veronica told her. 'Had to go out on some business. Is there a message?'

'Yes. Will you tell him that I have to go to Albany for a few days. My father has to have an operation, and they've called for us to come down tomorrow.'

'I see. Albany. Your brother, too?'

'Why of course. Harry and I and Papa. Will you tell George?'

'I certainly will, Michele.'

Mickey nibbled her lip after she put the phone down. What sort of business could George be transacting on a Sunday night in a little village like Miller's Gap? There wasn't any answer—any acceptable answer, that is. And why was Veronica so interested in whether Harry was coming along, too? All in all it was a very quiet meal that night, and Mickey excused herself early to pack for

Papa and herself.

The helicopter arrived right on schedule. Mickey had never
flown, although there had been opportunities aplenty. She
sat through breakfast with a nervous stomach while the two
men laughed and joked their way round. She became so
nervous that when the first sounds of the machine were
heard she ran for the bathroom and lost all she had eaten.
Papa was his usual self, a carefully controlled ruin. Harry
spent more of his time watching over Mickey than he did
over the older man. So when they were all bundled in and
strapped down, and the machine jerked away from earth,
Mickey leaned against the coolness of the window-glass and
watched.

It didn't seem that they were flying. Instead, the world
was moving down away from them, and then speeding by as
they hung in one place. The reverberations of the huge
blades over their heads made conversation impossible. She
made one quick check of Papa Gregory. The patriarch was
enjoying himself immensely. Mickey turned back to the
window. Below, the verdant shades of the Forest Preserve,
two-million, five-hundred-thousand acres of land, stretched
in all directions, spotted with the blue of its thousand lakes,
and only occasionally a peep at man-made structures.
Hordes of people lived and died in the shadows of the park,
but little could be seen of their works. Instead the
helicopter was making friends with the mountain tops.
They hustled across Great Sacandaga Lake, flirted with the
bare bones of the Olympic ski jump, hovered over the old
race track at Saratoga Springs, and then the whole heart of
New York State lay before them.

Schenectady was to the west, where electricity was king

and the General Electric Corporation made its headquarters; Troy lay by the river, where once the world's largest shirt factory ruled, and where Sam Wilson, the meat packer of 1812 who, as Uncle Sam, was the origin of the cartoon characterisation of the United States, lay at rest in Oakwood Cemetery; and then came Albany, whose business was government, the capital of the state, whose Victorian charm had been overlaid by massive aluminium skyscrapers. They flew parallel to Highway 87, the Great North Highway.

They landed in Albany on a roof-top helicopter pad, and were whisked away to a suite already reserved for them at the Albany Sheraton. A suite for Papa and Mickey, that was. Harry had his own rooms on a separate floor. It was only eight-thirty. An hour and a half on a magic carpet had taken them from the middle of the wilderness to the heart of the cosmopolitan Capitol District.

The Albany Medical Center was within walking distance, but a limousine was waiting anyway. After an hour of rest and a second breakfast they were driven the short distance to the new centre. It was ultra-modern, meaning that admissions procedures for rich or poor were interminable. As the hospital attendants swept Papa into a wheelchair Harry and Mickey remained behind to fill out the ten million insurance forms that were required. By the time they caught up with the old judge he was tucked up in a hospital bed in a private room.

'There's no need for you both to hang around,' the patient dictated. 'I just get stabbed and checked and weighed and pounded. Nothing else is going to happen until tomorrow. Take the girl out to lunch, Harry.'

Mickey demurred, but could not stand up against two

Butterworth men at their most domineering. She kissed the old man, sniffed back a couple of incipient tears, and allowed herself to be shuffled outside. She ducked her head to climb into the limousine, thankful for the air conditioning, and paid no attention to their direction until they stopped at one of the entrances to Washington Park.

'We need to stretch our legs,' Harry stated, leaving no room for appeal. She followed him out into the brilliant sun. The Tulip Festival was a month behind them, but the park still bloomed with the massed displays of Holland tulips. It tied this, the first Dutch colony in the New World, back to its heritage. Henry Hudson, sailing for the Dutch East India Company, had brought his galleon, the *Half Moon*, this far up the river in 1609, looking for the Northwest Passage. When the Colonial Congress met here in 1754 Ben Franklin had proposed the idea of a Federal union. But in modern Albany, it was just hot. Mickey was grateful for the air conditioning when they returned to the car.

Their next stop was on State street, at Jack's Restaurant. She was grateful, too, for Harry's arm, supporting her into the air-conditioned interior. They found a table near the windows, bright in the sun in contrast to the subdued dimness of the remainder of the place. When he held her chair back she dropped into it, emotionally exhausted. His strong hands rested on her shoulders, gently massaging for a moment. She arched her back and brushed at the loose braid of her hair as he went to the other side of the table.

'It's a routine operation,' he chided. 'Come on, now, where's all that bravery?'

'I think I left it in my bag,' she quipped. 'Right next to my brains.'

'Come on now, Mickey, that was only a joke. At least it was supposed to be. Let me see a little bit of a smile.' She managed to turn up the corners of her mouth. He duplicated the motion. 'A little farther,' Harry prompted, expanding his own to an ear-splitting grin. It was too much. She throttled a giggle or two, but then everything got away from her. Laughter and tears shared her face at the same time, uncontrollably. He made soothing noises, and waved the waiter away. The whole affair lasted hardly two minutes, but did her a world of good.

'What would you like to eat?'

She waved the menu away. 'You choose, Harry. I'm really too excited to eat.' And besides, you always choose the best and most unusual things available, but I'll never tell you that. Some day some other lucky woman will, but not me.

'They have some of the finest seafood in the nation here,' he said, thumbing through the menu. While he conferred with the waiter her eyes wandered around the half-busy room. It was really too early for lunch. But back in the distant corner there was a figure—a familiar figure. One that did not care to be seen, evidently, for it was hiding its face behind a menu card. Face or not, there was no disguising who it was.

'Harry?' He held up a cautionary hand while he finished dictating their order.

'What is it?'

'Over there in the corner. I'd swear it was Veronica!'

He half turned in his chair and squinted. 'Too bad they don't light some candles,' he muttered. 'For all the fancy decorations you'd think they would. I can't tell, Mickey. Do you want me to go over and enquire?'

'I——Not on my account,' she sighed. 'Do it if you want to.'

'Me?' He chuckled and leaned back to allow the waiter to place the soup. 'Why in the world would *I* want to talk to her? This is a special cream of asparagus soup they make locally.'

'You——I thought——It's delightful.'

'What? The soup, or Veronica?'

'The soup, silly.' She spooned her way through the thick creamy liquid with gusto.

'You don't have to overdo it,' he laughed. 'Smacking the lips is not considered *de trop*.' She blushed, and set her spoon down.

'I—I only talked to her yesterday.' She did not want to talk about Veronica, but she had to solve the puzzle or her mind would give her no rest. 'I wonder how she got down here so fast?'

'Probably because she works here,' he offered. 'Finish your soup and stop worrying.'

'It's finished. The soup, I mean.'

'But the worry isn't?'

'Well—I——How did you know she works here?'

'Pretty basic,' he chuckled. 'I asked her. She does freelance work for a photo magazine.'

'I didn't know that.'

'How would you? You never read that sort of magazine.'

'Harry, stop teasing me. What kind of magazine?'

'A girlie magazine, of course.'

'Oh!'

'And there in one word is trial, judgement, and conviction,' he murmured. 'It must be your upbringing.'

'Well, if it is,' she returned indignantly, 'it's all your

fault. Who else raised me?'

'Not counting my father and your mother, are we?' She blushed again, and dropped her eyes to the empty plate.

'I didn't mean——'

'I know what you mean.' His hand came across the table to rest on top of hers. 'We were all pretty moralistic, were we? Old-fashioned?'

'I never minded, Harry,' she returned quickly. 'I never minded. And I don't now.'

He squeezed her hand. 'Good. Eat up.'

During the conversation her soup plate had disappeared, to be replaced by a salad plate, featuring thin slices of smoked salmon surrounded by lettuce, and a tiny mound of potato salad crowned by a stuffed olive. Her fork moved automatically. 'But what would she be doing here?' She was like a little puppy, worrying a slipper. 'There aren't any magazine publishers around this part of the city.'

'Who knows.' He shrugged his shoulders. 'I did mention to her once that this was my favourite eatery in Albany. But I doubt if she's chasing me.'

'Huh! A lot you know,' she said grimly. 'You'd think that lawyers would have a better-developed sense of survival. She's hunting you, Harry. And I won't——'

'Whoa,' he chuckled. 'No more schemes, Mickey. I'm a big boy; I can look after myself. I'm a hunter myself, with plenty of experience. You are *not*, I repeat *not*, to get me involved in another one of your stupid little schemes. Do you read me?'

'Yes, Harry,' she promised herself, and went on with the meal.

The dessert was slow in coming, and Mickey would not abandon a three-scoop banana split for love nor money, so when Harry consulted his watch and made some garbled statement about an important business telephone call, she waved him away and continued her attack.

He had been gone no more than three minutes when she looked up to find Veronica slipping into the empty chair. 'Mickey, how charming to meet you here. What a surprise! You don't mind if I join you for a moment, do you?'

Huh, surprise! Mickey told herself fiercely. She dropped her spoon and mutely waved permission. 'I don't see how you dare it,' the blonde prattled. 'Look at that mound of calories you're diving into!'

Mickey looked down, startled. She never had measured good food in calories, only taste. And her well-exercised body absorbed it all, processed it, and hardly varied half a pound no matter what she ate. 'Harry's spoiling me today,' she muttered, picking up her spoon again.

'Of course he is. You need to be spoiled. Your father? He's well?'

'They don't operate until tomorrow,' she reported quietly. There was no getting around the obstacle. Veronica meant to talk to her, even though the ice-cream melted away into a wasted puddle. 'He's well. What is it you want from me?'

'Want from you?' The elegant woman across the table waved away the attention of a passing waiter, and lit a cigarette. It was the most unmannerly thing Mickey could imagine, flooding a table with smoke while people were still eating, but she held herself back. There still might be something to learn, for Harry's sake.

'Advice, I suppose,' the blonde mused. 'I think I'm falling in love with your brother, Mickey. I could use all the advice I can get. And you've been so close, all these years.'

'You mean you want to marry him?'

'Why of course, love. I spent the morning looking over wedding gowns. Harry doesn't know it, but you realise that men are slow about marriage, and have to be prodded.'

'I—I don't know all that much,' Mickey offered, 'but I think you need to be careful. Harry is—such a domineering man. If you marry him you'll find yourself snapping to on command.' The woman across the table shrugged her shoulders.

'And he has a terrible temper, you know. Terrible. He smashes things, and throws things, and like that.'

'But he has his good points, too?'

'Yes. Even though he's my brother I can't overlook his good points. He's very even-handed—most of the time. And when he's in a loving mood—well, you'd know about that, I suppose. And you don't have to worry about his drinking. He has that under control.'

'He has a drinking problem?'

'Well, not now.' Deep in the middle of a new scheme, wrapped up in the picture she was improvising, Mickey leaned across the table and lowered her voice conspiratorially.

'It was that woman, you know.'

'What woman?'

'About five years ago, when he was just starting his law practice. She drove him to drink, and then he beat her up, and they——Well, Papa Gregory had a terrible time keeping him out of jail.' And God forgive me for telling such lies. God? The deity was not broadcasting on her channel right at the moment.

Veronica leaned back in her chair, moulding her figure-tight sweater in practiced ease, and blew out a long puff of smoke. 'Terrible,' she commented, but there was a gleam of something in her eyes. 'But a woman could put up with a great deal with all that money in sight, I suppose.'

'Money?' Mickey's mind went blank. She had no prepared ammunition for this kind of assault. 'You mean his legal income?'

'Well, there's that,' Veronica laughed. 'Is he a good lawyer?'

'Hardly,' Mickey rushed in, crossing her fingers on both hands. 'Why do you suppose he had to set up in Boston instead of here where the family name is known? The judge has to send him a monthly allowance to help him keep his head above water.'

'Ah, well, that's not important,' Veronica laughed. 'The judge, I hear, is worth some considerable amount of money. He's not well, and Harry is his only son. I suspect we might have to make do for a time, but sooner or later all that lovely money will just fall right into my lap. Right?'

And there we come to the bottom line, Mickey told herself. If I let her go on thinking such a thing, she'll snag Harry for sure. If I tell her the truth, God knows what will come of it! It won't make any difference to George, of course, but——The argument was lost before it began. What she knew might just be thrust in the balance for Harry. Knowing it all, Veronica might pass him up and look somewhere else for her next victim.

'I'm afraid I have to disappoint you, Veronica,' she condoled. 'When Harry graduated from law school his father gave him all the share of the family money that was due him. He spent it all, naturally, but there it is. I'm afraid that Harry—well, liquor and gambling did him in.'

Mickey had managed, for the first time, to breech that fortress of sophistication. Veronica looked startled, confused, and then froze her face into an unreadable mask. She toyed with her half-smoked cigarette, crushing it out in the saucer of Harry's coffee cup, and immediately lit another.

'If not Harry?' she prodded. 'He's the only son.'

'And I'm the only daughter,' Mickey announced proudly.

'You? Half a million dollars?'

'I suppose so.' Mickey sighed, doing her best Sarah Bernhardt imitation. 'But who's counting these days?'

'Who, indeed.' The lithe blonde rose from her chair with a new look on her face, and almost knocked Harry over in her concentration.

'Veronica,' he said genially. 'What a surprise!'

'Yes, indeed,' the blonde returned as she darted out of the restaurant. Harry turned to watch her go, then resumed his seat, shaking his head.

'What was that all about?' he asked.

'I don't know,' Mickey lied blandly. It was a terrible thing she had done, she knew, blackening Harry's character like that, but it was all in a good cause. 'Maybe something she ate didn't agree with her,' she continued. 'Do we go back to the hospital now?'

They did, but late that night in her bed at the Sheraton the dream came again, changed this time. The presence came, but brought a feeling of brooding sorrow with it. All in all, it was a more frustrating time than any of the others.

CHAPTER SEVEN

'AND on the third day he finally rose again.' Papa Gregory laughed. He was sitting up in his hospital bed, sipping at a paper cup of orange juice.

'That's almost blasphemy,' Mickey commented, studying him from every angle. Despite his pale white skin, his starved appearance, his fragility, he looked considerably better than before his operation, and full of cheerful devilry. It was just as well that Dr Philbert came rolling into the room at that moment. The little round doctor was puffing.

'Damned elevators don't work right,' he complained, mopping at his brow.

'It wouldn't be such a problem if you lost a little weight,' his patient commented. Mickey backed out of the way. There was no sense in being a rowing-boat stuck between two battleships, especially when they were firing salvos at each other.

'So now I've got another expert,' the doctor groaned. 'How are you?'

'That's what I pay you to find out,' the judge retorted. 'If I ever had a lawyer appear in my court with your attitude——'

'I know,' the doctor laughed. 'Sit still, damn it.'

'Your stethoscope is ice-cold,' Papa Gregory grumbled. 'When do I get out of this place? The food's terrible!'

'Stop grumbling. If you were twenty years younger I'd let you go tomorrow. But——'

'But you need the money, isn't that it?'

'To tell the truth,' the doctor admitted. 'I do. My fourth son graduates from college next year. It's expensive. Stick out your tongue.'

'What do you need to look at my tongue for? It's my gall bladder that you took out. It *was*, wasn't it?'

Dr Philbert ignored him entirely, addressing himself to Mickey. 'Lucky he had you to look after him,' he said. 'Any operation on a diabetic patient is difficult, but you've had him toeing the line, Mickey. Let him simmer for a few more days. Say, until next Wednesday.'

'And then?'

'And then you'll take him back up in the woods, where it's peaceful. Moderate diet, a little exercise every day—that sort of thing. I could send a nurse, I suppose. Know a lot of them would like a week or two up in the park with only one patient.'

'I don't need one of your nurses,' the patient grumbled. 'I've got Mickey to take care of me. Who needs more than that? Tell him, Mickey.'

'Papa, maybe we could talk after the doctor goes on his rounds?' Philbert heard his cue and took it, flapping out of the door, his long white coat unbuttoned, his stethoscope swinging down haphazardly from a pocket.

'Pill-pusher,' the judge yelled after him. And then, more quietly, 'The best damned surgeon in the state. Plays a lousy hand of poker, but he's good with that scalpel.' He settled himself back into his pillows, a smile on his face. 'Now, about that talk?'

She walked nervously around to the other side of the

bed, and dropped into the hard hospital chair. 'I had a telephone call last night,' she said. 'From George.'

'Ah. I see. And what did he have to say? Beyond the mushy stuff, of course.'

Her cheeks turned fire-red. There hadn't been a minute's worth of "mushy stuff". 'It's long distance,' George had said. 'I have to get right to the point.'

'All right. What is the point?' She could not help it if she had sounded wounded—put upon. Things had been too confusing all week long and, all her worries about Papa, George had definitely taken a back seat.

'I came into some money,' he had said hurriedly. 'We don't have to wait. Let's get married right away, Michele.' She had done her best to force enthusiasm. It was hard work.

'And so you see,' she told Papa Gregory, 'I can't make him wait too long. Perhaps a week or two?' A hesitant question. And I don't really know, she told herself, whether I want Papa to say yes or no!

He leaned back against his pillows. A shutter seemed to have fallen over his eyes. They looked at her now, blankly. And then his smile came back. 'Slow on the uptake,' he apologised. 'That's always been one of my problems. Well now, I always knew I would lose you, Mickey, but was never willing to accept it. So now's the time. Very well.' He stretched out one hand to stroke her unruly hair. 'When the doctor comes back I'll arrange for a nurse to come along with us. You want to be married at Miller's Gap, I suppose?'

'Yes, I suppose so,' she sighed. 'Something very simple.'

'In which case,' Papa said jovially, 'what the devil are you dong sitting around here? Get yourself out and buy a dress, girl. It'll be my wedding present. Harry knows all the stores. He can take you.'

'No, not Harry.' She could feel unwelcome bile welling up from her stomach. Her wedding dress? Certainly not Harry! It was a problem, mustering up a smile for Papa, then going downstairs to find a taxi.

Finding a dress was much more simple. She went down tothe Empire Plaza, found a boutique, and stated her needs.

'I want a dress for a wedding.'

The sales lady broke out in a wide smile. 'Of course, a wedding gown. We have a wide selection.'

'No, you don't understand,' she said desperately. 'I want a dress for a wedding, not a wedding dress. Something—a white suit, perhaps. Blouse, skirt, blazer?'

The argument had taken them through the lunch hour, but she came out with what she wanted, a plain white silk shirtwaister that came just below her knees, with a tiny ruffle of Belgian lace at the collar, and a thin summer jacket to go with it. Shoes she had in abundance. No veil, no coronet. Just the basic me, she told herself fiercely as she struggled to find another cab. What you see is what you get, nothing more.

Harry had been briefed before she met him back at the hotel. He was sitting in the living-room of the suite, nursing a glass of brandy. 'So there's going to be a wedding,' he announced. 'That the dress?'

'Yes to both,' she sighed. 'My feet hurt. The shops are all air conditioned, but when you step outside again it seems twenty times warmer than normal.'

'So do I get to see the dress?'

'No.'

'No? Just no?'

'Yes. What would you like for supper?'

He juggled his glass, took a sip, and stood up. 'I'm no sure,' he returned. 'I thought I had a date tonight, bu Veronica seems to have disappeared from the city. Nobody knows where she is. You wouldn't know anything abou that?'

'Me?' she squeaked, nervously adjusting the fall of he skirt. 'How would I know anything about Veronica?'

'Because you may very well be the last one to have seer her alive,' he said melodramatically. 'At lunch the othe: day. What the devil did you say to her?'

'Me? Say something to Veronica?'

'Like a broken record,' he chuckled. 'You're a lousy liar Mickey.'

'I am not!' she muttered angrily. 'I—I mean, I don't lie What a thing to say!'

'I wouldn't put it past you to lie like a trooper if you thought you could scare Veronica off,' he said. 'Still trying to arrange my life for me, Mickey?'

'No I'm not,' she snapped, 'but you need somebody to d it for you. You're like a little minnow swimming around next to a barracuda. If you don't have help those jaws are just going to snap and cut you off at the pockets, Harry Butterworth!'

'Well, thank you for your concern,' he said seriously. She checked both his eyes before accepting the words. Both were blank.

'That's what a sister is for,' she muttered. 'What did you want for supper?'

'Fried crow,' he called after her as she fled. She couldn' find any crow on the menu, but there was a small chicken Mickey called room service and ordered.

* * *

By Monday of the following week Dr Philbert confirmed Papa Gregory's release for Wednesday. On Tuesday morning, despite Harry's protests, Mickey left Albany in a hire car and started off on the drive back to the lake.

'It's a stupid thing to do,' Harry insisted as he leaned through the open window of the Mercury. 'Wait until tomorrow, and we'll all go back by helicopter.'

'Sure we will,' she complained. 'And we'll bring Papa straight out of the hospital into an un-aired house, where the sheets will be damp, and dust lying around on everything—oh, what's the use of talking to you? Somebody has to go on ahead, and I'm the somebody.'

'Just can't waint to be reunited with your boyfriend?' He was laughing when he said that; laughing everywhere except with his eyes.

'Well, yes, there's that, of course.' She shrugged her shoulders, started the engine, and motioned him away. It wasn't really true. She hadn't given George a single thought up until that moment, but if she had stayed a moment longer Harry would have realised—and laughed. She gunned the engine a couple of times as a final hint, then threw the car into gear and spurted off. As she watched through her rear-view mirror he walked a couple of paces up the drive, staring at the car, his hands on hips. Pure anger, she told herself. Thank God I'm going away for a day!

Her route took her west up the New York Thruway to the old city of Amsterdam, then northward on Route 30, along the west side of Great Sacandaga Lake. She was in the heart of the old tribal lands of the Six Nations, the land of the Mohawks, the guardians of the Eastern Gate into the land of the Iroquois. But it was a land no Mohawk would

have recognised. A dam had flooded whole valleys, making
Sacandaga Lake, the largest in the park, into a reservoir
Past a series of small towns she wandered, until finally sh
turned west again at Benson, and rattled and bumped down
the road to Miller's Gap. She pulled up at the house jus
before four o'clock under a tear-laden sky, as
thunderstorm rolled down the chain of mountains and
lightning stabbed at trees too proud to keep their head
down among their neighbours.

The trees around the house bowed her a welcome as the
twisted in the storm. She made a mad dash for the veranda
happy to be back, and opened up the house, despite th
rain. A few drops more or less would never harm the ol
wooden floors, and she did so much want to know the swee
smell of summer rain as she worked. A quick sandwich an
a can of beer sufficed. Afterward it was all work as she wet
mopped her way around. Dry dusting would not do; i
merely re-arranged the motes of dust, spraying the air
Along with his other problems, Papa was developin
allergies. So the wet mop, hard work, and enthusiasm. An
a room had to be opened and cleared for the nurse. By te
o'clock that night she was on the second floor, covered with
perspiration, when the doorbell rang.

Her hair was up in an old rag, her man's shirt was soake
clear through, and her denims would have disgraced a wino
but she went downstairs anyway, and threw the door open
There was no regard for safety; crime had hardly reache
into the woods as far as Miller's Gap. And ther
was—George.

'Mickey! I couldn't wait another day!' Along with th
quick lip came the quick embrace. It hardly seemed lik
George at all. She pushed away from him, into the ligh

and stared. He was dressed in his usual best, a picture of sartorial splendour in what was supposed to be country clothing.

'I'm—I'm all wet,' she protested.

'So what?' he laughed, reaching for her again. There was that curious compulsion that she had felt more than once lately, that fierce quick little argument in her head. He's your fiancé. Before you know it you'll be married, you and George. You owe him some response. She moved forward into his arms gingerly, and offered her lips.

'I couldn't wait,' he repeated, ushering her back into the house. 'As soon as I heard you were on the way back I had to come back myself.'

'You were away, George?' Her sense of pride had returned. Like a good hostess she led him across the living-room and steered him into one of the comfortable upholstered armchairs.

'Up in Watertown,' he returned. 'But I couldn't stay away.'

'Coffee, George?' He waved it off. She sat down on the couch opposite him, hands folded primly in her lap, and waited.

'The wedding,' he started off abruptly. She did her best to hide the dismay. 'I thought we could do it next Friday?'

Her mind churned. Today is Tuesday. Next Friday. Well, why not? 'Yes, if that's what you want,' she agreed, trying to force some enthusiasm into her voice. 'But I thought you wanted to wait until my twenty-first birthday? That's still almost two weeks off.'

'No, I don't want to wait,' he insisted. And then, more anxiously, 'Your family is agreeable to all this?'

'I—I think so,' she said. 'At least, if they're not agreeable, they're not against it. Does that matter?'

'Well, of course it does,' he said hastily. 'Wouldn't want to start off on the wrong foot, would we? But that does cause a problem.'

'Starting off on the wrong foot?'

'No, starting off before your birthday. You would expect me to take care of you after our marriage.' A statement, not a question.

'Of course,' she murmured.

'In that case then,' he chuckled, 'I need to have you sign this.'

'This' was a very legal-looking paper, a Power of Attorney. No girl grows up in a two-lawyer family without learning a thing or two by osmosis. Power of Attorney was one of those things. If she signed the paper she was giving George full legal authority to act in her name. And as she scanned the document she could see it contained no restrictions. Everything. And that's what it means, giving yourself into a man's hands, she told herself. But her mind told her something else. She had no right to sign such a document until her birthday. Until then, Harry was her guardian and trustee. But if George wanted it so badly, her mind asked? Reluctantly she scribbled her name across the bottom, and added the date, less than two weeks hence, when she would be twenty-one.

He had eyes only for the signature, not the date. With a flourish he waved the paper in the air, rolled it up neatly, and snapped an elastic around it. 'There now.' He sat down beside her on the couch with a very self-satisfied smile. That takes care of everything, Michele. Now don't forget, Friday morning, ten o'clock, at the village church.'

He's another male who thinks I'm a complete idiot, she

sighed to herself. I suppose he'll send me a reminder in the mail? Dear Mickey, we're to be married tomorrow at ten. Be sure to wipe your mouth, and tie your shoelaces carefully! She stirred uneasily under the weight of his arm. He took it for a hint, and got up.

'I have to run. A matter of business. You know how that is.' One chaste hiss on her wet brow, and he headed for the door.

'No, I don't know how that is,' she muttered as the door slammed behind him. 'What a time to come romancing, when I'm all sweaty and tired and—and I haven't finished upstairs.' She managed to stand up on creaking legs, and hit the stairs. There was something nagging at her, something she could not put her finger on. George. He seems a lot like Harry when he's up to some shenanigan, she thought but what in the world could *George* be up to? He's nowhere near as clever as Harry. Let's face it, a genius the man I'm going to marry is not. Now Harry—that's a different story. But George has *something* going for him, she reminded herself as she bent her back to the work. He certainly is the best-looking man I've ever seen!

As a result of all her work the house gleamed at nine o'clock the next morning when the helicopter announced itself with a roar. The skies had cleared, and it landed in brilliant sunshine. Papa Gregory got out slowly, unassisted. Harry preceded him, and he was followed by an elderly woman in white. Mickey, who had been holding her breath, released it all. The nurse was a quiet little white-haired lady, full of smiles and laughter.

'I was expecting you'd bring one of those young curvy ones,' Mickey murmured to Harry as they watched Papa come up the path.

'Purely business, Mike,' he grinned. 'I don't believe in mixing business with pleasure.'

'The heck you don't,' she gave him a verbal jab. 'How's Veronica these days?'

He was standing on the bottom step of the veranda, watching his father, while Mickey remained on the top step. He turned his head up in her direction for a second, flashing that big smile. 'What great big teeth you have, Grandma,' he murmured, and then turned around to offer a hand to the judge.

'I don't need any help,' the older man snapped, almost out of breath. 'Mickey—well, maybe I do need help. Give me an arm up the stairs, son.' He clumped up the stairs one at a time. Mickey came down two steps, and slipped under his other arm. His big hand squeezed her shoulder. 'Missed my girl,' he grumbled. At the top level he went over to the swing and settled down in it. 'Took more breath than I expected. Mickey, meet Mrs Parker. Ann, this is my daughter, Michele.'

The two women smiled at each other over his head. Mickey could feel the instant rapport. 'You need some rest, Mr Butterworth,' the nurse insisted. 'That's a long adventure for your first day out of hospital.'

'Your room's ready,' Mickey coaxed.

'Of course it is,' he grumbled. 'I don't want *two* women haunting me.' And then the Butterworth smile came out. He's doing that on purpose, Mickey told herself. Trying to charm us both at the same time, and getting away with it. She flashed another quick look at Ann Parker. The nurse was smiling, but there was a gleam in her eye that revealed she knew the score. Between them they helped the old man up the stairs and into his bed.

'Can't even let me undress myself,' he grumbled, and then wiped away all the protest with a loving squeeze of Mickey's hand.

'You know something, Papa?' she said. She was the last in the line going out of the room, and she stopped at the threshold. He smiled at her expectantly. 'You're an old fraud,' she giggled, and ducked out of the door as he made threatening moves with his pillow.

Harry was waiting for her when she came down. He took her hand and towed her out to the veranda. 'Any news from the home front?' He patted a space on the swing, in offer. She settled down beside him, her face glowing.

'He doesn't want to wait,' she told him. 'George wants us to get married on Friday. The day after tomorrow, that is. Down in the village chapel. I think he has everything arranged.'

'I thought the bride's family did that,' her brother chuckled. 'Doing it simple? It'll save us a bundle of money. How about a reception here afterwards?'

'Why, that would be nice, Harry!' She hugged his arm and kissed his cheek. 'Now what more can a girl want?'

'A coach and four? A glass slipper?'

'Please don't say that. Not even as a joke,' she returned soberly. 'I don't want to be a Cinderella. That bit about midnight, and the horses turning back into mice—that scares me. I want this to be happy for ever and ever.' I want it to be simple. It can't be perfect; I'm marrying second-best, and I know it. I don't want wild excitement—just peace and quiet. And someone to grow old with.

'It will be if you wish it so,' he promised solemnly, and patted her knee. 'I think I have to run in to Gloversville,' he continued. 'There's a fellow there I want to talk to. You'll be OK?'

'I don't see how I could get in trouble,' she assured him. 'Not with Ann taking care of Papa. I think I'll just sit here and daydream.'

'A girl's entitled to that,' he agreed. There was a tiny pause, as if he wanted to say something more. Then, instead, he ruffled her hair gently in his old familiar manner, and sauntered down the stairs.

Mickey folded her feet up under her, her mind only partly tuned to the little incidental noises from inside the house, where Mrs Parker was making preparations and setting up an office for herself in the kitchen. A girl has a right to daydream. Funny, all she could dream of was a succession of faces. Veronica, George, Harry, Papa Gregory. One after another their pictures flashed stage centre, and were almost immediately erased by one to follow. Over and over the pattern repeated, and always the same. Veronica first, then Papa, then George, and finally Harry. His face would linger for a second or two longer than the others, and then the rotation would start again. she shook her head to clear her mind. Veronica? Where had she disappeared to? Was Harry really safe from her predatory ideas? Papa? Was he really safe and happy? There was a deep-throated grumble from upstairs, followed by laughter for two. Papa and his nurse, going at it. They seemed to get along fine, so that should take care of that.

Mickey lay back in the swing, content to let things go on without her. Behind her, in the house, the telephone rang. The nurse apparently was too busy to pay it any attention. At the fourth ring Mickey lazed herself out of her comfort and ambled inside to answer.

'Michele?' A woman, on the verge of panic. Veronica.

'Yes.' Not much of a display of welcome for her prospective cousin-in-law, but Mickey had run out of niceness.

'Mickey, I'm calling long distance from New York city. I can't seem to reach George at home, and I need to talk to him urgently. Is he with you?'

'No, he's not here, Veronica. I haven't seen him today.'

'Mickey, it's really urgent. Can you try to find him and give him a message?'

The woman had Mickey's interest now. 'Of course I will. Wait while I find a pad and pencil.' She set the phone down and hurriedly ransacked the desk. 'OK, go ahead.'

The woman at the other end was having trouble formulating the message. 'Tell George I had a call from—from the loan people. Yes, loan people—he'll understand. They've found a problem with the paper that George gave them—are you getting this down?'

'Yes, but go a little slower. The loan people—what next?'

'They claim there's a real problem about the date on the paper George showed them, and they're very angry. Very angry.'

'Yes, I have that. Anything else?'

'Oh God, it's stupid.' Cool-headed Veronica was whimpering down the telephone line. Something had frightened her very badly. 'Just—just tell him to be careful, that's all!'

'I have it all,' Mickey promised. 'And to be careful. I'll see if I can find him.' The line went dead at the other end. Mickey sat down on the arm of the chair next to the telephone, nibbling at her lip. George had done something foolish. He must be warned. Mind made up, she decided to try the telephone first, and dialled his number. The instrument rang ten times before she put in down. And now what?

George still had to be warned. If he wasn't at home, she had to go and leave a note for him. Just the thought startled her. George had been courting her since early spring, and not once had she ever gone to his house. A small rental affair, he kept saying. 'Nothing like the house we used to own. I would be embarrassed to have you see it.' That was the turn-off. In the fragile first months she had had no wish to embarrass him. But this was urgent.

Ann Parker was back in the kitchen. 'Your father's asleep,' she said. 'I thought I'd make some tea.'

'Do that,' Mickey laughed. 'Make yourself at home. I have to run an errand.'

'No problem. He'll probably sleep for two or three hours. Is that a beach down there?'

'It sure is, Ann. But don't forget you're in the mountains.'

'I've never been in the mountains. What does that mean?'

'It means wear your fur-lined bathing suit,' Mickey called back over her shoulder. Her car responded at the turn of the key. She backed carefully on to the driveway, and started on her search.

George had rented the Lovetts' old house; she remembered it vaguely. The dirt road that followed the lake front had not been maintained since Hoover was president, and her car bounced and strained every spring it possessed in that thirty-minute trip. The house was actually a summer cottage: five or six rooms, with minimum plumbing, and no insulation at all. It stood all alone about twenty yards back from a tiny beach, up the side of a hill. There was not a sign of life, discounting the squirrel running up one of the tall pine trees that shaded the area.

She pulled her car off the road into a dry patch that looked as if it had been used for parking many times. With the motor turned off, the silence became deafening. An occasional bird cried in the distance, but nothing stirred in the immediate area. She walked up to the tiny front porch. 'George?' She had no hope of an answer, but called again anyway. A crow, high up on the mountain, screamed raucously at her. The noise was startling.

'There's no sense standing outside and scaring yourself to death,' she muttered. The door yielded at the turn of the knob. And why not? This isn't Albany, she reminded herself. Feeling like some sort of housebreaker, she edged her way inside. 'George?' No answer.

The doorway gave directly into a small living-room. It was about what she had expected. A few scattered chairs, none of them looking particularly comfortable. The sort of place that was rented as is, furnished, for people who intended to spend most of their time outdoors. A staircase led upward. Behind it the living-room seemed to curve off around a corner. She followed the curve into a modest kitchen.

Dishes were piled everywhere. The tap in the sink dripped steadily. Unconsciously she tried to turn if off, with no success. George was just not a very neat housekeeper. She shrugged her shoulders. Neither was Harry, and he was the man against whom she measured all men. Leave Harry alone in an immaculate house for three days and he could make a pigsty of the whole place, and that by hardly trying. George appeared to be his equal.

She grinned at the thought. Sloppy husbands were probably the norm in America. She rubbed her hands on an almost-clean towel, and walked back to the living-room. Leave a note, her logical mind said. She sat down at the little table in the middle of the room and started to write. Luckily she had brought her own paper; there didn't seem to be much to offer in the little house. When she shifted her weight slightly the chair under her creaked ominously.

'Get up before you fall down,' she lectured. The chair creaked again. She pinned her note down on the table top, using a half-empty beer can as a weight. Poor George. At least I can give him a clean house, she thought. How about that for a great marriage objective! There was no need to conceal the wry smile; there was nobody available to notice.

'You might as well look over the rest of the house,' she told herself, and started for the stairs. They, like the chair, creaked. But the banister seemed sturdy enough, so she clung to it and went madly on.

There was a hall of sorts on the upper floor. On the right was a small cupboard, masquerading as a bathroom. It had all the fixtures, and she knew it must work, for the tap up here was dripping as well. Back out in the hall she walked down to the far end, where the light of a window helped her to see. The door to that far room was closed. She forced it open; it scraped, and then jammed against something. She peered around the jamb. The entire room was crammed with junk: all the left-over peices of furniture no longer worth renting, all crammed into one eight-by-ten room, waiting for Judgment Day.

Still smiling, Mickey came back to the only remaining room. At least this one looked habitable. A bed, a chest of drawers, a cupboard with its door half open. The bed was queen-size, but had not been made up recently. Two of the drawers in the chest were open. She shoved them closed and wandered over to the wardrobe.

It was crowded. All of George's fine casual clothes, and two of Veronica's dresses. Not exactly a fair share of the space, she noted. I hope I can do better when I live with George. There was nothing else to see. She made her way back down the rickety stairs and out into the fresh air. A small breeze had sprung up, toying with the flood of wild flowers that peppered the mountainside behind the house. Mickey stretched, breathed deeply, and headed for her car. There was nothing else to be done.

Total concentration was required on the drive home. The road was so poor that an instant of inattention would put her into a ditch, so it wasn't until she was back at the Devlin house, parked in the shade beside her brother's car, that a thought struck her.

Veronica and George shared that house. They had shared it for three months—so George said. The clothing in the wardrobe seemed to confirm it all. There was only one bedroom; only one bed. Somehow it didn't quite surprise her. Mickey walked into the Butterworth house in a very reflective mood.

CHAPTER EIGHT

'YOU'RE very quiet tonight.' Harry came out of the house late on Thursday with his coffee mug in his hand and joined her, sitting on the top step of the porch. She shifted to one side to make room, settled her skirt again, and rested her stubborn chin on her fists. 'Not talking at all? Last-minute regrets?'

'I don't want to talk, Harry.'

'All right.' He draped one arm casually over her shoulders and sipped from his mug. The evening was fading into night. The sun was already behind the western mountains, but there was an afterglow that clung to the lake. She had been thinking all day. Stubborn. Mule-headed. Those are the only words that apply, she though fiercely. If you had the sense God gave little children, you'd call the whole wedding off, go jump in your car, and be five hundred miles away by tomorrow. And that would just about break Papa's heart and the vow you made to Mama. Look after him? Lord, I've been nothing but trouble to him! Nothing but.

And then there's Harry. If I don't marry George, Veronica will have clear sailing with Harry. If I do, I can continue to put a spoke in her wheel, put her off until Harry comes to his senses and finds someone suitable.

So what about George? Well, you knew he wasn't perfect when you first accepted him. Think of all the millions of women who have married before this, not necessarily for love. For their families rather than themselves, or for money, or for politics, or a host of other reasons. It can't be all *that* bad, can it? And probably George is the unknown face in my dreams. And I promised. It's too late to figure out the puzzle about two people and one bed. It's too late for anything. And so Mickey Devlin Butterworth will go down the aisle tomorrow, and become Michele Armstead. And the world will keep rolling on, and probably nobody will start a nuclear war, and the man I love will never know what I've done, or why I've done it! A tear started at one corner of her eye. She masked it quickly with a handkerchief and a fake sneeze.

'Allergy, huh?'

'I guess so. Harry?'

'What?'

'Papa won't be able to walk down the aisle with me tomorrow, will he?'

'No chance of that. But we did bring a wheelchair. He can get around. I think Mrs Parker could bring him in for the ceremony.'

'I——'

'Go ahead, ask. Why did you think I came out here, anyway?'

'Darn you, Harry Butterworth,' she snarled. 'You really would steal candy from babies, wouldn't you!'

'That's more like it,' he chuckled. 'I don't feel right when my little hard-headed firebrand mopes around. Yes I would, if I liked the flavour. But you wanted to ask me a question, and I was afraid you were going to become a dying swan right in front of my eyes. What's the question?'

'Would you—Harry, would you walk me down the aisle?'

'And give you away?' She looked up quickly, caught by the agony in his voice. The darkness had moved in one them; she could not see his face.

'Yes,' she whispered.

He cleared his throat, and squeezed her shoulder gently. 'Yes, of course I will,' he sighed. 'After all, what are brothers for?'

She leaned over against him, rubbing her nose into his pale white shirt. He held her close for a moment or two, and then stirred and got up.

'I think I'd better take a walk,' he announced. She made to get up beside him, but his hand on top of her shoulder held her down. 'Alone, Mickey,' he added. 'I've got some serious thinking to do.'

She watched until his familiar figure faded into the gloom, and then went down to the water's edge herself. The star pattern was brilliant overhead. She snatched up a handful of pebbles from the little beach, and scaled them, one at a time, out over the water. Once, when she was ten, she had scaled a rock for four skips, and crowed like a fool when Harry made only three. The memory brought a wry smile. She dusted off her hands and made her way slowly back up to the house, and the dishes waiting in the kitchen. She was still musing as she showered and prepared for bed.

'Tomorrow the world will be different,' she murmured to herself as she braided up her hair. 'Tomorrow I'll start a new life. After tomorrow there'll be no turning back.' The thought was no comfort. She tossed and turned, and when she finally dropped off to sleep it was a nervous, fitful affair. And when she woke up in the morning, the world hadn't changed a single iota. It left a leaden feeling in the pit of her stomach.

* * *

Mickey went down to breakfast in her robe. Mrs Parker was a morning person, and had already prepared Papa's breakfast. The two men were dawdling at the table, nursing mugs of coffee. 'Well, you look more like Hamlet's ghost than a blushing bride,' Papa commented. 'Couldn't sleep?'

'Nervous,' she admitted. 'Tossed and turned all night. . .'

'Happens to all brides,' the nurse interjected. 'Want me to make you some eggs?'

'I couldn't eat a thing,' Mickey protested. 'My stomach is unsettled.'

'Your mother was like that,' Papa Gregory said. 'Couldn't eat a thing all that day when we were married, and then got totally drunk on one glass of champagne at the reception.'

'That's a lot of comfort,' Mickey returned sadly. She dropped into the chair. A mug of coffee appeared in front of her. She looked down to see Harry's hand withdrawing, and flashed him a smile of thanks. The mug warmed her hands; it was the beginning of July, and she was shivering.

'Everything's set for the reception,' Harry announced, trying to get her mind off her troubles. 'We've catered for it. It's eight-thirty now. Mrs Parker will drive Papa down to the church at nine-thirty; you and I should leave at nine-forty-five, and after that, it's George's problem.' His warm hand dropped lightly on to her shoulder and squeezed.

'Synchronise watches?' she asked feebly, trying to stir a smile. Harry's hand moved from her shoulder to gather her two palms together.

'Be happy,' he commanded. He seemed to be having trouble with his voice. It quavered at the end of the statement.

'And for goodness' sake, be dressed,' Mrs Parker interrupted. 'You've barely an hour. If you're really not hungry, why don't we go upstairs and get you prepared?'

There wasn't all that much preparation to be made, but Mickey was thankful for the suggestion. She trailed along up the stairs behind the nurse, and lost herself in making what she might of her small resources.

'The dress fits well, and looks well.' Mrs Parker was bustling around Mickey as if she were a patient. 'Simplicity is the best style for you, Michele. And pure white goes with your hair. But I had expected——No veil? No hat?'

'I didn't want anything fancy,' Mickey murmured.

'But you have to have something on your head, dear. I know it's going out of style, but for a wedding? St Paul, wasn't it—women in church should cover their hair? Or something like that. I didn't study too hard in Sunday school. And I never had hair like yours. I've known men who would kill to possess a girl with your hair!'

'Now you're really putting me on.' Mickey was gradually shaking herself out of her gloom. It might have had something to do with 'clouds and silver linings', but she could not remember how the rest of that old saying went. 'You don't think the dress is too——' She made a vague gesture to her bustline. In the shop it hadn't seemed to be all that conspicuous.

'Perfectly all right,' Ann told her. 'If you've got it, show it. Isn't that the old saying? What better time to tease a man than at his own wedding? But we really have to do something about—I know. Here, let me zip you up, and then I'll run down stairs and—well, you'll see.'

She bustled for a moment or two more as Mickey sat quietly on the bed. She had braided her hair and fastened it up in a coronet. Her dress was immaculate. Her little white court shoes made a lucky match. She was as ready as she could ever be. Mrs Parker dashed for the door. Mickey checked her watch. Nine-fifteen, and time for Papa to leave.

She got up, brushed down her skirt, and headed for the stairs. Harry had already loaded Papa and his wheelchair into the limousine. Nurse Parker was standing at the front door. 'How about this for a headpiece?' she offered.

Mickey looked and was pleased. The older woman had taken one of her amber plastic headbands and plaited flowers from the garden around it, to make a fairy queen's crown. She bowed her head so Ann could slide it on.

'Just right. Now you look—pure innocence, dear Mickey. Isn't it strange, I can't keep from crying, and I have to run. God bless you, child.'

'I can't seem to stop, either,' Mickey sighed. She stood in the open door and waved as the limousine pulled away. Papa Gregory was leaning out the window, applauding, as they disappeared around the stand of oak trees.

'You're letting all the flies in,' Harry said as he came back up the porch to join her. 'Can't keep your powder dry? You'll have to do better than that, Mike.'

'Harry, I'm scared.'

'Of course you are, love.' He was too sombre to be the teasing brother she had known all these years. Sombre, comforting, and perhaps just a little distant.

'Want to talk? We have fifteen minutes to kill.'

'On the swing, Harry? I'd like that.'

He escorted her out and closed the door behind them. She settled into the swing carefully, to keep from creasing her dress. He stood for a moment, just in front of her, hands in his pockets, and then sat down beside her. It's just an old habit, she told herself as his arm came around her shoulders.

'It will be the quietest wedding I ever attended,' he commented. She had been staring down at her hands, folded quietly in her lap. Now she looked up at him. He was staring out over the lake, expressionless.

'I thought it would be best.' I haven't anything to celebrate, so why should I need help doing it? she thought.

'Not even a bridesmaid?'

'No. Not even.'

'Lovely day for a wedding.'

'I'll miss all this, Harry. Seeing the world from our front porch and all.'

'Oh? I thought perhaps—I have all the papers ready, Mickey. As soon as the wedding is over you'll take over everything your mother left you. I had thought you and George would want to live here, considering that dump he lives in now.'

'Oh, no.' She turned to him in panic. 'This is Papa's house. He loves it. It'll always be his. I don't know what George plans, but we won't force Papa out of his own house.'

'Your own house, Mickey.'

'His house.' A firm statement, made with determination, with her little Irish chin stuck out, defying the world.

'Then of course we'll pay you rent.'

'Harry! Are you trying to insult me? Rent a house to my own father?'

'All right, all right. I'm sorry. I can't seem to keep my tongue in order. We'd better go.' He stood up and helped her to her feet. He hesitated and twice started to say something without making a sound. They walked over to the stairs. She took his arm, as she always had. Harry stopped her. 'Mickey, are you sure?'

She answered quickly, not daring to delay for fear of what she might say given a moment to think. 'Yes. Of course I am.'

He nodded his head gravely, and escorted her down to his big car.

Harry drove slowly, guiding the vehicle with one hand while the fingers of the other tapped interminably on the steering-wheel. There was no traffic in town. A solemn quiet settled over everything. Even the birds were still. 'Where do you suppose everyone is?' he asked.

'I don't know.' She leaned forward to look around him. The only sign of life was Hughie Patlen's dog, a ten-year-old bitch with a torn ear, whose hunting days were long behind her.

The little wooden church stood at the far end of the village, at the point where Main Street became Route 309 again. It occupied a triangular plot of grass, with a little path in front, and a small graveyard at the back; Miller's Gap, a summer resort, had little call for burying. The building was as plain and simple as the New England Congregational churches from which it was copied. A bell-tower set squarely in the centre of the front was the tallest structure in town. The bell bayed a slightly off-key welcome as Harry pulled up at the front door.

They sat like a pair of statues after he turned off the motor. A susurrus of sound swept out from the church and overwhelmed them; the secret of the empty village was solved. Every able-bodied man, woman and child was inside, waiting.

'Sort of like the lions waiting for the Christians,' Harry muttered. 'Shall we get out?'

She pressed her lips tightly together and nodded. He

climbed out, slamming the door behind him, and came around to help. She was so immersed in her own dreams that she hardly noticed. Harry was tiger-tense, looking for something to smash, but trying to restrain himself. He slammed her door as well. One of the deacons, standing in the open door of the church, made 'hurry up' motions. Mickey took her brother's arm and they walked slowly up the four stairs, and on to the porch of the church.

She pulled him to a stop before they went in. 'Harry,' she hissed, 'don't do it!'

'I thought that was my line,' he said. 'Don't do what?'

'Don't marry Veronica!'

'Still managing my life?' He pressed hard against the hand she had placed in the crook of his arm. 'You needn't worry, Mickey. I'd never marry second-best.'

It was too late to ask him what he meant. The organist occupied a loft directly over the main doors of the church and sat with her back to the altar, with only a rear-view mirror for her cues. Mrs Patterson had been playing that organ for forty years. Partial deafness made her enjoy her own playing all the more. Someone up at the altar had given her a signal, and the old organ gasped out the solemn music. As if compelled, Harry started off slowly down the aisle, and Mickey was forced to go along with him.

Mickey's world went out of focus the moment they crossed the threshold of the church. The pews were packed, but she didn't notice. Papa Gregory was sitting in his wheelchair at the very back of the church, but she failed to see him. There was a roaring sound in her ears. She fought desperately to stay in control. Her legs moved automatically. The organ thundered. She clutched at her brother's arm as if he were her last refuge.

Half-way down the aisle a thought struck Mickey and left a sudden pain. This would be the last time she walked anywhere on Harry's arm. All those years were moving behind her, all those pleasures. She was stepping out of girlhood into a world of uncertainty. George—handsome, sloppy George. They would have such beautiful children, that was what everyone in town kept telling her. The thought dug into her like a sharp spear. She struggled to hold back the tears that threatened to engulf her.

Veronica; think of Veronica, she snarled at herself. Think of Papa! A shadow had just appeared between herself and all her yesterdays. A shadow blocking out the light, blocking out reason. She felt Harry come to a stop. She did, too. He kissed her gently on the forehead. Somewhere in the distance she heard him murmur again, 'Be happy, Mickey.' Then he passed her hand into George's, and faded out of her line of sight.

The ritual was as old-fashioned as the church, straight out of the Book of Common Prayer, and the King James Bible. She heard it all, but not clearly, and not closely. When George went down on his knees at the chancel she followed. The words flowed over her head. Leaning back slightly, she had finally located Harry out of the corner of her eye. He was kneeling in the front pew, all alone, staring straight ahead, looking like a graven image. She gulped down another tear. Mickey Devlin Butterworth, a child of tempers and responsibilities, love and laughter, had come to the end of her tether.

George nudged her, bringing her back to her senses. The whole church was quiet. The minister, solemnly robed in black, was standing directly in front of her, looking at her with a smile.

The stillness did not disturb the Reverend Mr Stample. He had married more than a thousand couples in his ministry, and was prepared for almost anything. There was a twinkle in his eye as he repeated, 'Do you, Michele Devlin, take this man to be your lawful wedded husband . . .' The words faded out as Mickey's brain began to function.

Why, he's got the wrong man, she told herself fiercely. Do I take George? She turned her head slightly to look at the man kneeling beside her. Charming, handsome, debonair George? She leaned back slightly again, looked the other way, and caught a glimpse of Harry, still kneeling with hands clasped in the pew to her left. Mr Stample was looking at her again, smiling that deep warm smile that made him such an effective pastor.

Do I, Mickey, take this man? In the silence of the church her answer came loud and clear, pitched higher than her normal contralto, like the voice of some child awakened suddenly from a bad dream.

'Good heavens, no!'

She stood up, dropping George's hand. Mrs Patterson, leaning forward into her mirror, saw the movement at the altar and the organ thundered into the triumphant wedding march. The congregation, seeing the movement, hearing the organ, stood up too to watch the processional. Mickey stalked up the aisle as the organ thundered. George stood at the altar, his handsome face marred by an astonished look. Someone was walking behind Mickey. She refused to look. The number of mouths open in the congregation, multiplied by 3.1416, Mickey muttered hysterically to herself, would reach the moon!

At the end of the aisle she saw the wheelchair, and almost stopped. Dear God, what have I done to Papa? she thought.

What have I done! Her knees buckled. She caught herself with the aid of a hand at her elbow.

Papa Gregory was sitting in his chair, a broad grin on his face. 'That's my girl,' he said as she staggered by him. 'You left it a little late, but better late than never. Your mother would be proud of you!'

Mickey was out in the sunshine before she understood the words. Mother would be proud of her? It seemed so improbable—but who would know better than Papa? She needed that unrecognised hand which guided her back to the car, opened the door, and helped her in. Seconds later the driver's door closed gently. Her eyes were downcast, toying with the little bunch of daisies Mrs Parker had pressed on her.

'Harry?'

'Yes?'

'I've really messed it up, haven't I?'

'I wouldn't say that.'

Mickey took a quick look back up at the church. Mr Stample was standing in the doorway, his Bible clutched in his left hand up against his chest. She could read his lips. 'Good heavens,' he was saying over and over again. George was standing beside him, his lips pressed angrily together, his fists clenched at his sides. She turned her head to watch her almost-husband as Harry started the engine and drove them swiftly away.

The drive down to the church had taken fifteen minutes; the return trip was accomplished in six. The tyres squealed as Harry slammed on the brakes and they skidded to a stop in the parking area. As they had at the church, they sat side by side, frozen in position, like a tableau. She *had* to break the silence.

'Harry——' she started to say.

It was as if she had turned the key on a waiting bomb. He turned to her, grabbed her by both shoulders, and shook her until her head was about to unhinge.

'God,' he snarled. 'Listen to me, Mickey Devlin. I—am—not—your—brother!' He gave her one more shake for emphasis, then pushed her back into the corner of the seat, climbed out of the car and stalked up to the house, leaving her all alone in her misery.

It was difficult to stop the shivering. The sun had found an opening in the interstices of the trees, and was baking the roof of the car. With the motor off and the air conditioning not functioning, the interior was slowly becoming a sauna bath. She sat there, shaking, twisting her fingers into each other. The door of the house slammed again. She looked up. Harry had changed into denims, and was stalking off towards his favourite walk, the path that wandered along the lower slope of the mountain. She watched his back until he disappeared into the trees. *I am not your brother!*

She gasped at the pain of it. It was as if she had sinned against all the race of men, rather than just against George. Harry had cast her out. Of all the sorrows she had to bear this day, nothing could match this—that the brother she loved so desperately had disowned her.

Wearily, moving like an eighty-year-old woman, she edged her way out of the car and trailed up on to the veranda. Behind her, down the drive, she could hear the motors of several cars. In no mood to explain or defend herself, Mickey fumbled her way into the house and up the stairs to her room. Not until the bedroom doore was firmly closed behind her did she feel safe.

The cars outside halted. Doors slammed. At least half a dozen voices, all happy, were making conversation, but too far away for her to understand. Mickey leaned back against the bedroom door, clenched her fists, and fought against the quivering muscles that were rendering her impotent. The noises from outside shifted into the house. One of the voices was the rumble of Papa Gregory. A woman was giggling.

'Get a grip on yourself, Michele Devlin,' she muttered. The command worked. Her muscles relaxed and stopped their terrible St Vitus' dance. Feeling almost as if she had just completed a marathon, totally exhausted, Mickey managed to reach her bed. She dropped down on it, gasping for breath. The soft mattress enfolded her. She lay back, letting familiarity soothe.

'The downstairs party increased in volumne. More chatter. There were at least four women there. Their voices carried above the counterpoint of the men. Mickey shook her head to clear the cobwebs. A party to celebrate the terrible mess she had made? Not possible. But what else could it be? 'This is my wedding day,' she told herself fiercely. 'You fool! There were a hundred reasons for going through with it, and not one of them valid!' Harry's words at the church door came back to haunt her. '*I'll* never take second-best.'

The little dress that she had bought for the day restricted her. She sat up, managed to stand, and wiggled herself out of it. It fell to the floor. Almost unconsciously she picked it up and began to fold it neatly. The wind through her window toyed with her slip as she stood there, dress in hand.

'Shall I tell George?' became 'What shall I tell George?' as her mind flashed from one option to another without cease. Someone downstairs turned on the stereo. She could hear the clink of glasses being raised. 'I'll never tell George

anything,' she almost shouted. Her mind had circled
enough; the search was over. 'And I'll never marry second-
best either,' she declared firmly to the empty room.

The neatly folded dress seemed to be burning her hands.
Mickey opened her fingers gently and watched as the soft
silk floated to the floor. And only then, in controlled anger,
did she stamp on it and kick it into the corner. The tears
flowed.

An hour later, dressed in an old blouse and jeans, she leaned
back against her doubled-up pillows. The Devlin eyes were
red but, beyond that, there was no evidence of the
cataclysm which had taken place. The party downstairs was
still on, becoming more enthusiastic as time passed.
Michele shook her head, a wisp of a smile playing at one
corner of her mouth. The knock at her door startled her.

Mrs Parker stuck her head through the partially opened
aperture. She wore a broad grin on her face, and held a glass
of champagne in her hand. 'Ah. Your father wondered
where you were, Mickey.'

Michele swung her feet to the floor and snatched the
flower-decked headband off. It tangled in her mass of hair,
and destroyed the neat little coil. 'I don't—what are they
doing down there?'

'They're celebrating, love. All your real friends.'

'Celebrating? After that fiasco? I can't believe
they——What are they celebrating?'

'Well, your father gathered them all outside the church,
love, and invited them to come home with him for a "get
well party".'

'Get well party?'

The elderly nurse came across the room to the bed and

offered the glass. 'You have no idea, Michele, how very much your family and friends wanted you not to marry that man. Now, go splash some water in those eyes and come down.'

'I couldn't do that, Ann. I'm just too embarrassed to be seen in public. I just can't.'

'Your father wants you. It's no good hiding up here in a corner. You can't hide for the rest of your life. You've just had a terrible shock. The only way to recover from it is to throw it all off and come downstairs.'

'My father wants me?'

'Yes. The party is all his idea.'

Well, at least Papa Gregory hasn't turned his back on me, she told herself. I can't hide for ever. She relieved the nurse of the champagne glass and aquired a little Dutch courage.

The two women came down the stairs arm-in-arm, to be greeted by a welcoming shout. It was all true; her real friends in town all gathered round and toasted her. Papa Gregory wheeled himself through the crowd to her, and held out both hands.

Mickey dropped to her knees in front of his chair, clutching at his hands for strength and comfort. 'Papa?' Her eyes asked the rest of the question.

'I'm very happy at how it turned out,' he comforted, 'And your mother would be proud of you. Very proud!'

'Proud?' She was like a penitent, beating herself with chains of her own making. 'How could anyone be proud of a fool? I could have stopped it earlier, but I hadn't the nerve. I thought I could be satisfied with George. And when I found out I couldn't I just didn't know what to do!'

He leaned over and pulled her forward to where her head

rested against his chest. One of his hands ruffled her hair, reducing it to total chaos. 'You did the best you could,' he murmured. 'If your mother had been here it would never have happened. Now you have only one more piece of business to take care of, and then you can put it all behind you.'

'One more——I don't understand.'

He tilted her chin up and studied her grey eyes. 'George,' he said solemnly. 'He's not the man for you, but he deserves an explanation.'

'I don't think I have the nerve to do that,' she returned.

'Not this minute, Mike. Right now we party. Tomorrow you can explain.'

'Papa?'

'What now?'

'Harry hates me.' Her voice fell off at the end, losing the last word in a dry sob that shook her body.

'Hates you? What makes you say that?'

'He—he was so angry that when he drove me up to the house he shook me, and yelled at me.'

'Exasperated, love, but not hate. What did he say?'

'He didn't say. He yelled. "I am not your brother!" he yelled! I think he would have given me a good knock if he—— I think he hates me, and he doesn't want me for a sister at all, and I feel so——' The tears again. Ten thousand gallons. The party guests eddied away, trying to make believe nothing was happening. Papa Gregory sat quietly, patting her hair, until the storm was over. When she lifted her tear-streaked face, the old man was smiling.

'Of course he doesn't want you for a sister,' he chuckled, 'but that doesn't mean he hates you. Come along now. One of you people bring my only daughter another glass of champagne!'

CHAPTER NINE

GEORGE finally arrived at about four o'clock on Sunday afternoon. Mickey was helping Papa Gregory take his daily walk. Helping, that is, by being a crutch to him, held against his side by his strong right arm. 'I don't really need a wheelchair,' he told her. 'It's just that yesterday, with the crowd and all, Ann thought it would be the better part of valour to use one.'

'And it gave you a sense of importance,' she teased as she guided him around a root-outcrop. She had slept late and long, soothed by three glasses of champagne. Of all the family Mickey had always been the one with the lowest capacity for alcohol. And so someone—she didn't dare ask who—had put her to bed. No headache ensued; instead she came downstairs at noon feeling rested, relieved, almost rejuvenated. Lunch had been a simple salad. Harry had not made an appearance, and Mickey didn't dare to ask about him. And now here was Ann to interrupt.

'There's a man come to see you, Michele.'

'Somebody we know?' For some vague reason she had expected a day free of visitors.

'I think so. He was at the wedding. A big tall man, blond, good-looking.'

'George,' Papa grumbled. 'Wouldn't you know.'

'I—don't want to talk to him,' Mickey muttered.

'You have to,' Papa said firmly. 'You owe him an

161

explanation, at least.' In the distance, over the mountains, a thunderstorm was gathering. Papa's voice sounded just like one of those strokes of thunder: firm, striking, demanding. He gave her shoulder a gentle shake to reinforce the words.

'All right,' she acquiesced. 'I don't know what I can say, but—he deserves the right to yell at me, I suppose.' She slipped carefully out from under Papa's arm, and was supplanted by Nurse Parker.

George was waiting for her on the bottom step of the veranda, coming out of the house when he heard their voices. He was not his usually handsome self. His hair wanted combing, his shirt was wrinkled, and his face was set in a peculiar expression that Mickey could not read. 'I need to talk to you,' he snapped, taking her hand in his. 'Not here.' He looked around to where Papa and the nurse were slowly approaching. 'Down at the dock.'

She hung back, not saying a word. He towed her across the grassy lawn, and out on to the float. 'George, please. You're hurting my hand!'

'Not as much as you hurt me,' he returned. 'Get into the boat, Michele.'

'I don't think I want to,' she started in protest. He glared at her, and almost pushed her off the pier. There's no sense protesting, Mickey told herself. He means to do his yelling in private, and he has the right. She sidled out of his way, perching herself up in the bow so there was no way he could force her to share a space.

George didn't even try. He went to the stern, cast off, and started the little electric outboard. They puttered away, out of the cover into the depths of the lake, turning north along the chain of tiny islets. It gave her a good time to study him, something she had never really done in the three months of their courtship. His cheeks were flushed, he obviously hadn't shaved, and that cocky debonair look that marked him from others had disappeared.

I must be dreaming, she told herself. Where has all that handsomeness gone? He looks as plain as Harry. Maybe even more so. What's been the matter with me all this time? I feel about George as if he might be my brother, not my husband. He looks like a man who needs mothering. Is that what I've been hung up on all this time? George needs a mother? That's what I would have been if I'd gone through with that crazy ceremony—his mother, no less!

It was there, right in the middle of the lake, that she rediscovered an old truth. One that she had always known, but had kept hidden—from herself? If my love for George is stricktly brotherly, what about my feelings for Harry? She knew, just as if one of those threatening clouds had thrown a lightning bolt straight at her heart.

'I am not your brother!' Harry had said, shaking her madly in the car yesterday.

'He doesn't need a sister!' Papa Gregory had commented yesterday, when she cried in his lap.

And deep in the mist of her memory, Mickey could see herself with Mama, standing on that very wharf on Mickey's fourteenth birthday. Mickey Devlin, full of the fun of life, preening her newly acquired curves, boasting her adolescent breasts. And her mother, calmly lecturing. 'You can't have everything in the world that you want, Mickey. Harry is your *brother*. Don't ever forget that!'

Mickey hadn't. All the years she had not forgotten. All those years she hand gone to bed at night and thanked God for giving her Harry as a brother. All those years she had loved him with all her heart, and felt uneasily guilty about

it. *Harry is not my brother!* She felt so excited about he
discovery that she wanted to tell somebody, but George wa
not the one.

They were well clear of land when he shut down the
motor and came up to the bow, squatting on the seat facing
her. Well, here we go, she thought. She squared he
shoulders and prepared for the barrage to come. It did, bu
not in the fashion she had expected.

'You *have* to marry me,' he pleaded. 'By tomorrow
noontime.'

'I can't do that, George. I don't love you.' No more roon
now for second-best; no place for argument.

'You *have* to,' he insisted. 'You have no idea what you're
doing!'

'You're wrong, George,' she said softly. 'For once in my
life I know exactly what I'm doing. I can't marry you.'

'Damn you,' he muttered. 'Why not?'

'I'm sure there are a million reasons, but I just told yo
the only important one. I discovered that I don't love you.

'Hell, you don't fool me! I've been watching the way you
suck up to that brother of yours. Brother! What a laugh
The way he looks at you, anyone can tell he sees you
without any clothes on. Is that the way it is with you two?'

Her hand flashed out, rocking his head back. He snarled
and pulled her off her seat into the well of the boat. She
glared up at him, her back wet from the water standing in
the scuppers. 'You have no right to talk about Harry like
that,' she snarled. Her fighting temper was up, as it always
had been when Harry was the butt of accusations. She
scrabbled to a sitting position. 'Let go of me, George.' He
turned her wrist loose reluctantly. She rubbed it, to reduce
the pain. Keep to the attack, her mind warned her. He's a

big man bearing a big grudge! She looked quickly around her. They were about a mile from any shore; about five hundred yards from Chamapan Island. A little far for a swim, but not entirely out of her capacity. Get him on the defensive, and if that doesn't work, go overboard!

'I was at your house on Thursday.' A conversational tone, couched in her gentlest voice. 'I always wondered, George, why you insisted that I shouldn't come to see you there.'

'So what?'

'You keep a very sloppy house, for one thing.'

'Now you're going to tell me you won't marry me because I keep a sloppy house?'

'Not at all. I just wondered at the housekeeping arrangements, that's all. I wondered how it is that you and your "cousin" Veronica could live in that house with only one bedroom—and only one bed?'

'I slept on the couch downstairs,' he grumbled.

'Come on,' she said disgustedly. 'There isn't any couch downstairs. And there were the marks of two separate heads on two pillows upstairs—on the one bed. So just who is Veronica?'

'I told you. She's my cousin.'

'A number of times removed?'

'What's that got to do with it? We weren't married, you and I.'

'Maybe, George—but how about you and Veronica?'' His face turned beet-red; almost it seemed that his head swelled up. Anger and frustration—and perhaps fear—destroyed the beautiful symmetry of his face.

'So she's my ex-wife,' he roared. 'So what? Are you trying to make a criminal case out of it? I'm not married now, that's the important part.'

'You never said a truer word.' she returned. 'You're no
married now. And you're not going to be—not to me!'

His arm drew back half-way. Mickey suddenly concluded
it would be a good idea to have some space between them.
She struggled to her feet, rocking wildly as the rubber
bottom of the boat shifted under her heels. She almost
pitched overboard. Had it not been for George's strong
arm, she might have hit the water. It wasn't exactly a
rescue. He held her roughly around the waist, then dragged
her to the stern and slammed her down in the well, in front
of the aft thwart.

Mickey made one more lunge to get away from him. He
caught her arm, twisting it cruelly behind her back, forcing
her down again. She struggled on, but every twist she made
brought further pain to her trapped limb. The truth was
slow to penetrate her flaming anger, but it finally did.
Strength would not serve her now. She allowed herself to go
limp.

The pressure on her upper arm relented, but George
maintained his grip. He muttered under his breath as he
used his other hand to re-start the motor. Once more the
little boat puttered down the lake, pitching slightly as the
waves increased.

The thunderstorm no longer hovered over the mountain
peak; it moved swiftly towards them, towards the lake. She
knew the danger. 'Get us ashore,' she yelled at him in
panic. George was a man with multiple worries; his grim
face reflected something more than anger. But anyone who
has lived at a lakeside learns quickly. An isolated boat or
person in the middle of the water during a lightning storm
has a high chance of being struck. That knowledge leaked
through. He turned up the throttle and directed the little

rubber boat towards the nearest islet. Chamapan, it happened to be, the island where Papa Gregory had established a fishing-lodge in those long-ago days. She prayed as they raced for shelter. It was one of those contests where Mother Nature almost wins. They had hardly beached the boat and run for the forest when a massive bolt came flashing out of the heavens, smashing into the tall pine tree at the landing, and splitting it all the way down from its towering hundred-foot peak to its scattered roots.

'We're lucky we were so close to the island,' she gasped as they ran.

'Not luck,' he grunted. 'I meant to come here all along.'

The rain came after the lightning. Not a tender summer rain, but one of those all-out assaults, with drops big enough to drive holes in the mud of the trail. Panic brought opposite reactions. George was muttering to himself, pushing her ahead of him up the trail, almost mindlessly. Mickey gradually grew in strength as the wild tympany of the storm raged around her head. They stumbled up to the log-cabin structure. There was no lock on the door. George gave her an extra push that sent her sprawling in front of him, her head almost in collision with the old Franklin stove in the corner of the one-room lodge. She rolled up in a ball to catch her breath, and then rolled over and sat up. George was standing at the closed door, leaning on it, his body shaking with dry sobs.

Mickey used the cold iron of the stove guard to pull herself up. Her hair dropped down over her face like a wet shroud. She gathered its ends together in one massive handful and wrung out some of the water, then fished in her pocket for a piece of string with which to tie it back. And all this time George stood at the closed door, unable to react.

His condition presented Mickey with a problem she was not sure she wanted to solve. As long as George was confused like this he could certainly do her no harm. And she felt a tug at her heart, a tug that held her because, no matter what else George might be, he *was* human. Undecided about what to do next, she sat down on the double bunk bed built against the far wall, and waited. Gradually his weeping spell broke. He turned around to her, a pathetic appearance of a man. The storm, his earlier upsets, had washed away all the glamour, and left him an empty shell.

The swift-moving storm gave them two more salutes of thunder, and passed on south, looking for more worthwhile game. The world outside was reduced to the constant drip of a forest which had more water than it could hold. Somewhere outside the door a tree was dripping on to an old abandoned wash-bucket. The metallic clang was a torture.

She waited for him to say something. Or do something. He was the man; it was his responsibility. But George just stood there, shaking.

Mickey went over to the door. The centre of the storm had gone, but it was still raining outside. They were isolated, but in no real danger. 'We can't go back,' she told him. 'Not until this storm lets up. We need a fire.'

George turned to the wood pile and fumbled. Mickey watched, then went over and relieved him of the job. The lodge was a fishing shelter, but also a refuge for any passer-by caught in a storm. Wood was always kept available, and a box of matches. On a little shelf above the stove were a few cans of food. Kindling and paper were stored beneath the bunk. It took some doing, but a fire was finally blazing.

Within ten minutes the top of the old Ben Franklin stove took on a glow, and heat began to circulate. George crowded her away from the stove and warmed himself.

Mickey shrugged her shoulders, glad to be out of his way even if only for a moment. She wandered over to the single window. It faced out on to the path that led downhill to the boat landing. Occasional glimpses of the moon were showing through wind-tattered clouds. The rain had stopped. There had to be a way to talk George into co-operation. She moved back towards the fire.

'The storm is over,' she said softly. 'We'd better make some move towards going back. Everybody will be worrying about us.'

He looked over at her. There was a nervous tic working at the right corner of his mouth. 'We're not going back,' he growled.

'Not going back? But——'

'Oh, shut up,' he snarled. 'You had your chance yesterday, Michele. Now it's my turn to call the tune. We're not going back until tomorrow. Or maybe even the day after.'

'I don't know what you think you're up to, George Armstead!'

'Don't you really?' He offered her a little sarcastic laugh. His nerves were coming under control. Even sopping wet, as was she, George was beginning to regain that godlike appearance. Mickey was using her fingers to comb out her dishevelled hair. George produced a comb from his pocket and went at his own locks.

Look at that, will you? she told herself. Fully prepared. He'd be the only man on the passenger list to have brought a life-jacket with him on the *Titanic!* Feeling very much like the unglamorous peahen in the presence of her lordly mate, she slouched down on the bed.

'Maybe you'd better tell me about this great problem,' she coaxed. 'Surely it wasn't being left at the altar that stirred you up to this extent. You were playing around with your ex-wife all the time you were courting me. After the Devlin fortune, my broth—Harry said. What a laugh that is!'

'What the hell do you mean by that?' He was over at her in a flash, holding her shoulders not too gently, his angry face looming over her like some predatory bird.

She sat up straight and mustered her courage. 'If that's what you were looking for, you're batting zero,' she blu out. 'The Devlin fortune has been a fake for forty years. My grandfather Devlin died broke!'

'Died broke?' There was anguish in him. It poured out from between the syllables as he spoke. 'Damn you Michele!'

It's getting to be a habit, she told herself dizzily. Everybody line up and give Mickey Devlin a good shake. 'Cut it out, George,' she roared. It was a bigger roar than the size of her could sustain. George was so startled his hands dropped away from her, and he took a step backwards. His fingers were still flexed into fists.

'Well, there'll be that other,' he decided grimly. 'Maybe they'll wait.'

'There'll be that other what?'

'The half-million you're going to inherit from your father. Now what are you laughing about?'

'So that's why Veronica disappeared from the scene in Albany? The pair of you decided I was a better target than Harry? I told her at noon. How long did it take for her to call you?'

'About an hour,' he started to say, and then halted in the middle of the last word. 'Don't try to put me off,' he growled at her.

'What's the matter, George? Losing your image? Surely you know what everyone knows around here. You don't have the brains to plan an operation like this. So it was Veronica behind it all the time.'

'What difference does that make?' he snapped. 'We were going to split the proceeds anyway.'

'I'll bet you were.' Mickey managed a little tinkle of laughter, just enough to turn his face red. 'Do you suppose she would honestly give you a share of the take, George?' The arrow hit home. 'And what did you plan to do with me?' And so did that one.

'Shut up.' He moved on her again, like a bear who poked his nose into a bee's nest before he could get his paw in. Alert to the danger, she dodged around the rough table which sat in the middle of the room. 'Shut up,' he repeated angrily.

'And what do you think you're going to accomplish by keeping me out here all night?'

He stopped. She could see hope gathering in his eyes. 'Michele, we were friends. We could be again. You don't know what a mess this is.'

'So tell me.' She backed towards the cabin door, a step at a time.

'I didn't come into any money,' he stuttered. 'I borrowed it from a group down-state, based on—certain guarantees.'

'Based on a post-dated Power of Attorney, George? What are these people? Bankers?'

'Not exactly. They—loan money.'

'And you took the money and ran?'

'Hell, no. I'm not that much of a fool. I took the money and *you* ran.'

'You mean they loaned you money because you were going to marry me? That's impossible!'

'No, it isn't,' he continued doggedly. 'They saw it as a very good investment. And they were willing to clean things up afterwards.'

'Clean me up, you mean?'

'No, nothing like that, Mickey. Nothing was going to happen to you! Dear God, I love you.'

'Yes, I'm sure you do,' she whispered. 'But you loved my inheritance just a little bit more. You brought me here intentionally, didn't you? Why?'

'Because I know your father's an old-fashioned man. I figured that if we spent the night out here alone like this, he'd demand a marriage, and everthing would be OK.'

'But not now?'

'You know too much,' he said bleakly. 'I thought we would be married before it all came unravelled.'

'Well, don't let it worry you, George. Even if it had worked you would have been out of the running. There isn't any money—not from me, anyway.'

His head snapped up again. She let the words sink in, and then continued. 'I'm not a Butterworth,' she announced. 'Papa Gregory's not my father; Harry's not my brother.' She could see George start to shiver, so she added the final coffin nail. 'And I won't inherit a cent of the Butterworth money. It was all a big lie I made up to scare Veronica off. She should have stuck to her original goal. Harry's worth a lot of money!'

Again she stared at him as he mulled over what she had

said. That was a nice touch, she told herself. Harry's not my brother! Now we have everyone saying it, so it *must* be true. Her confidence was increasing almost as quickly as her clothes were drying, but she had been too cocky, too sure.

Almost before her eyes George turned from a beaten man to an automation seeking vengeance. He gobbled in rage as he slammed the table out of his way and rushed at her. There was no finesse to the attack. He slammed into her and wrapped her up in a bone-cracking hug. She struggled, kicking at his ankles, freeing one hand long enough to scratch a bloody line down his face. He loosened one hand and slapped her hard high on her left cheek. She was hanging on the fringe of darkness, limp in his arms, when the door behind her bumped into her back and pushed both of them out into the middle of the room. And the voice she knew so well said, 'Am I interrupting something?'

CHAPTER TEN

MICKEY huddled in the corner, her arms wrapped around herself, trying to be inconspicuous. Somehow, in the past few seconds, she had been dislodged from the middle of the pile, and now the two men were standing nose to nose in the centre of the room, paying her no attention. 'Thank you, God,' she whispered. There was no place for her slender frame in *that* confrontation.

George was the bigger man; in all directions he exceeded Harry's size. But that hardly seemed to bother Harry. When he forced the door open George had Mickey trapped in a bear hug. One of Harry's hands had come over Mickey's shoulder, seized George by the throat, and walked the big blond man away from her as if it were all easy.

'Like to beat up little girls, do we?' Harry, with his most casual voice, dropped his hold and rested both hands on his hips, daring. George made an inarticulate sound and threw a right hook at his assailant. Harry weaved slightly to one side without moving his feet, and ducked. The blow went over his head.

'Nasty!' Harry stepped back a foot or two, his stance changing.

'Harry! Be careful!' It was meant to be a yell, but came out a squeak.

'Ah. Worried about me, are you, love?'

It all sounded so nice, but in that second that his eyes had shifted toward her, George had launched another right hand. Mickey screamed. Harry turned casually away from the blow, but as the first came at him, his own hands snatched at George's wrist, and very suddenly George was flying through the air over Harry's shoulder, to skid into the opposite corner of the room. His head struck the log planking with a satisfactory thump, and George Armstead collapsed.

Harry watched for a second, then walked over towards Mickey, brushing down his clothes as he came. She huddled back against the wall, astonished. This was a new side of Harry, one she had never seen before.

'You—you hit him!'

'I believe I did. Now, how about you?'

'Oh, I'm fine.' She felt terrible, to tell the truth, but all her young life she had always done her best to conceal such things. Harry knelt down in front of her.

'Yes, I can see how well you are,' he murmured. 'Just like that time I pulled you out of the lake. You were 'just fine' then, as I remember.'

It was almost enough to spark her off. Almost. 'I only spent a week in the hospital that time,' she sighed.

'Don't want to fight?'

'No. Not with you, Harry. I—I'm really not fine at all!' She ducked her head to hide the tears streaming down her face, but he was having none of that. He picked her up gently, hugged her close, then carried her over to the bunk and stretched her out.

'I can see you're not,' he said sombrely. 'That's going to be a beaut of a black eye, Mickey. Didn't your mother ever tell you not to play those sort of games?'

'Don't tease me, Harry.' A tiny flicker of compassion ran across his face and was quickly gone, washed out by his usual grin-and-bear-it look.

'No, I won't,' he told her. He sat down on the edge of the bunk beside her, and rubbed her wrists solicitously. 'I know you've had a hard time of it, Mike. It's all over now.' He rearranged her head in the middle of the pillow. Over his shoulder she saw movement, and screamed.

Harry was up like a shot. George had recovered, picked up the only chair in the room, and had come back to the attack. 'Don't watch, Mickey,' Harry cautioned. He stood between her and the attack, with his back to her. 'He wants to play rough again.'

She wanted nothing more than an excuse to squeeze her eyes shut, and pray. There was a startling crash, a movement of feet, another crash. The door came open. She could feel the breeze from it. Through it all she kept her eyes shut, squeezed as tight as her muscles would allow. Hey, God! her mind yelled. But of courser He is always watching. The Lord is my shepherd——Like echoes out of her childhood the words came back to her mind. She said them, and was comforted. The tears stopped. You can only be frightened to death for a minute, she told herself grimly. Then either you die or you get better! The cabin door slammed, and she felt a warm presence beside her.

'My, what a chicken you turned out to be.' There was no sting to the comment. The voice was comforting. His cool hand touched her forehead and brushed her hair back out of the way. She managed to open one eye.

'So there you are.' He stooped and kissed the eyelid. It fluttered, and the other opened. Harry's face filled her view, with no room for anything else. She searched his craggy face for signs of the fight. There was not a mark. He was breathing a little heavier than usual, and a lock of his thick brown hair had fallen down over his forehead, but his deep brown eyes were gleaming at her.

'George?' she croaked.

Harry had been leaning close; now he sat up straight and laughed. 'George decided to go home. He said something about another engagement. Or something like that. I wasn't listening too closely. He asked me to return something to you.' He pulled a crumbled paper out of his pocket and showed it to her. It was the Power of Attorney she had signed. Harry shook his head, made a 'tching' noise with his tongue, and tossed the paper into the stove. 'Dangerous, that,' he cautioned. 'Signing your life away!'

'You could have been killed!' She felt indignant about *that!* There's hardly any use in having your own hero if he gets himself killed.

'Don't tell me. If George had killed me you would never have spoken to me again!'

'Oh Harry, that's a terrible joke! It was bad ten years ago, and it hasn't improved with age! But yes, I would have been angry. He's so much bigger than you, and I——'

'You weren't half as worried as I was,' he quipped. 'If I had known what I was doing, I wouldn't have done it!'

She sat up on the bed and hugged him. Or as much of him as her arms would reach around. 'Shut up, you fool,' she groaned, 'or you'll have me crying again!'

'We can't have that, can we?' Mickey had never recalled how warm his arms were, how tender the holding of him could be. He crooned a nameless melody into her hair as he rocked her slightly back and forth. Her heart fluttered, but her pulse settled, until at last, comforted, she slipped out of his arms and stood up.

'See. I'm OK.' She did a little pirouette to demonstrate,

caught the heel of her shoe in a crack in the floor, and fell back into his arms.

'Mickey, you really need a keeper,' he cautioned her. But the arms cherished her.

'I suppose I do,' she reflected. 'I wonder if I should advertise the position?' She leaned back in his arms, far enough back to see his face. 'But there's one thing I know, Harry,'

'What's that?'

'I'm *not* your sister.'

Well!' It was a long sigh that accompanied the word. 'Thank God for little favours. It's been one hellish eight years!' He set her aside, and resurrected the table and the chair. It had only three legs left, so he pulled the table over by the bed. What did he mean by that? Eight hellish years?

'Come on, woman. Let's get something to eat. I'm starving.'

'Woman's work? Why don't we go home and get a decent meal?'

He gave her an astonished look, but it was overdone, and she knew it. 'Now what?' she asked.

'I do believe that George took the boat,' he said, and that broad grin returned. 'It seemed there was something wrong with his arm, and before I could stop him he went off. How about that!'

'Harry Butterworth!' She stamped her foot. 'You mean to tell me you let that big——' Stop talking, she warned herself, turning her back on him to keep him from reading her facial expression. This is Harry. There's always something up his sleeve. Go softly! Mickey took a deep breath and tried counting to twenty, backwards. It worked. She turned around again.

'Harry, how did you know where I was?'

'Do I have to talk on an empty stomach?'

'All right,' she grumbled, moving over to the food shelf. 'We have beans and frankfurters, or, if you prefer, frankfurters and beans—or, if you'd rather, just plain beans. And a can of spinach.'

'You chose,' he laughed. Her hand went out blindly. Beans and beans. She searched under the shelf for the old can opener and the single saucepan.

'You can talk while I work,' she commanded. 'As always. Women's work is never done, and all that.'

'That's because women never stop talking long enough to *get* it done.' He settled back on the bed in lordly fashion.

'No wonder you never got married.' She gave the can opener another twist, and the lid came off. 'And get your shoes off the blanket! Now, how did you know where I was?'

'Papa knew. I came back to the house just as you and George putted out of sight.'

'And you came right after us?'

'Not exactly. Don't burn the beans, please. I hate burned food. No, I gave it a little while, and then the storm and all——Well, you wouldn't want me paddling up the lake and catching my death of cold, would you?'

She slammed the saucepan down on top of the stove and walked over to him. 'You mean to say I was in danger up to my neck and you waited until the storm was over? Why you—double-devil, you!' Both her hands, like talons, reached for the one spot just under his ribs where Harry was ticklish. He roared uncontrollably and twisted away from her into the depths of the wide bunk. Mickey was poised to attack again, one knee up on the bed, the other on the floor, when his hands came down on her wrists and he pulled her in after him.

She landed on top of him with a thump heavy enough to drive the breath out of her. The laughter disappeared. It was

cut off in both of them as they lay nose to nose. A fine cloud of
her long hair fell around his face. His hands shifted to each
side of her head. In one blinding flash she knew the face of her
unknown lover! Her mind rocked at the revelation. Slowly he
pulled her down. She offered no resistance. When his lips
touched hers she could no longer be passive. She squirmed
against him, trying to make two bodies occupy one space,
pressing, questing, opening her mouth to the prowling of his
tongue. Someone was moaning in the distance. Her ears shut it
out. Shut out everything except for the glorious pain of the
assault. But just as suddenly as it had begun, he was thrusting
her away from him.

'And thank God I'm not your brother,' he said. She looked
down at him. His eyes were so big, so close, she could see her
own reflection in them. Soft wonderful eyes. Strong wonderful
Harry. So wonderful that he was—good lord!—almost
handsome. She felt something tugging at her heart.

'Harry?'

'Hmm?'

'You—didn't like that?'

He slipped both his hands under the back of his neck and
grinned. 'I liked that very much.'

'What did you mean, Harry, about eight hellish years?'

He thought for a moment. 'Your mother was the most
wonderful and the most astute lady I ever knew,' he explained.
'I don't remember my own mother, but Mama, nobody could
fool her. You'll remember when you were thirteen, I was
twenty-one?'

The arithmetic made sense to Mickey, but nothing else did.
She nodded her head and waited. Was he going to say the
word she ached to hear? Love?

'You were a very promising thirteen, Mickey, and I was a

college boy who thought the best things in life were free. Boy, did your mother ever put a stop to that. She really laid into me. Grabbed me by the ear, no less, and towed me away from the house. "Mickey doesn't need a lover, Harry Butterworth, she needs a brother!" Her exact words. I don't think I'll ever forget. "When she's old enough to choose for herself, then maybe you can re-think your relationship." '

'My mother?'

'Your mother. Well, I lusted after your cute little body for a couple of years, and then decided to be a whole-hearted brother until you were eighteen.'

'Lusted? Not——'

'Lusted. Until you were eighteen. And then—well—good lord, you're burning the beans!'

He gave her a quick little shove. She rolled off the bed and barely managed to rescue the pan, burning the tip of her finger in the doing.

Mickey did a little dance around the room, blowing on her finger while juggling the hot handle of the pan. 'Don't you dare laugh,' she threatened him as she found the top of the table and dropped the beans.

'Hey, I wouldn't dare laugh.' It was his favourite boy Scout tone: contrite, innocent, and totally fraudulent. He came up off the bed in one motion, like some jungle cat, catching her as she blew on her finger, soothing her. She smiled up at him, and then took one look at their dinner.

'That looks terrible,' she sighed. 'Why don't we go home?'

'I told you about the boat,' he returned. She stetched up on the tips of her toes and kissed his chin. It was the only target within reach.

'Pull my other leg,' she suggested. 'You didn't swim out here. I noticed very carefully how we abandoned the discussion right after you waited out the storm. Very cowardly, too, must say. How did you know I didn't need you at once?'

'I had confidence in your abilities,' he laughed. 'I figured that you'd get mad at him about eight o'clock, and would have chewed him up and down one side by nine-thirty.'

'So stop beating around the bush. How did you come?'

'In the damned canoe. I almost thought I'd just wait around so there I was standing on the dock when the light appeared out on Chamapan Island, and right away I knew you were in trouble. So I jumped in the canoe and paddled like Hiawatha and stormed to the rescue. Wasn't that wonderful of me?'

It was hard not to laugh, surrounded as she was on all sides by him, her head turned to rest against the steady beat of his heart. *I love you, Harry Butterworth,* she told herself. *I've loved you since I was fourteen years old.* 'That proves it isn't puppy love.' Mike clapped her hand over her mouth. She hadn't meant that to come out like that.

'What?' he queried.

'I said yes, that was wonderful of you. But you barely made it. Next time, don't wait so long.'

'Oh, I won't. That's a promise. So is this.' He backed her out far enough to bring his head over hers again, lips caressing at every point. She was up on her toes again, offering full co-operation. There was a flame of contact, a rushing cacophony of sound in her ears, a wandering of the spirit, and then again he put her aside. It took more time for her to recover after this one. She turned her back again until her breath came under control.

'So you see why we can't go home,' he said blandly.

She whirled around. 'I don't see any such thing, Harry. You have the canoe, the storm is over—and the more I look at those beans the less I like them. Why are you stalling?'

If it were possible she would have sworn his cheeks were red. Under the tan he had accumulated it was hard to tell. In any event, he shifted his eyes away. Watch it, she shouted at herself. Harry always said beware of the man who looks you straight in the eye. He's about to tell you the biggest whopper you ever heard in your life!

Harry tightened his grip around her waist and walked her over to the stove. 'You know,' he speculated, 'that George Armstead wasn't completely wrong in everything.'

She stopped in mid-pace. 'Good lord, I never expected to hear you say that! What is it that he was so right about?

'About Papa,' he teased. 'If he knew you were out here all night with a man he'd sure reach for the shotgun and call the preacher.'

'But—I don't understand. You mean you don't *want* to go back tonight? You mean you——'

'Love you? Want to marry you? I have for years, Mickey Devlin. I've always regretted that we never legally made you a Butterworth, and here's my chance to get it done right. Right? What the devil are you crying about now?'

'Love me?'

'Does that sound so impossible?'

'Harry—I don't know. It's hard to dig out the truth from between the smart remarks. You want to marry me just to get my name changed to Butterworth?'

He gave her a look out of the corner of his eye. 'That sounds so much better than my saying I still lust after your body, Mickey, and I want to jump on you?'

'Well, maybe. But that——There's still that bit about love and cherish, and things like that. A girl likes to hear that sort of thing, you know.'

'Yes, I suppose so,' he sighed. 'One thing they never taught in law school is how to come straight out with "I love you, Mickey, and I want to share the rest of your life. I want to settle down and raise a family, and——" God, that sounds sickening, but it's true. I've loved you since you were eighteen. I took one look at that saucy hair and those deep eyes, and discounted your bad temper and your wild scheming and your bossy attitude. Right then I decided I would wait for the most favourable time, and pop the question. I knew there was no use struggling against the tide; that I could never spend the rest of my life without you—and not as a sister, either. And then, good God, I came home and find you engaged to that—wimp! And on top of that I'm volunteered to give you away to him at the wedding! I could have killed you both. And myself, too, for that matter. Lady, I was sick to the stomach, walking down that aisle with you on my arm and George waiting there at the altar. I damn near threw you over my shoulder right then, and ran off with you.'

'You should have,' she answered quietly.

He grinned. 'Now you say that. In the church I prayed like mad that you'd come to your senses. When you did, I was so happy that—wow! Believe me?'

'Haven't I always believed you?' She lifted her solemn little face. He offered a tender warm caress. 'Except when you promised you——'His exact words came back to her. 'Darn you, Harry, you tricked me again! I asked your promise to help Papa Gregory come to like the idea of my marriage! You scoundrel!'

'Scout's honour,' he said solemnly. 'I meant every word of it. Papa Gregory is going to be ecstatic about your wedding. To tell the truth, that's one of the things he called me home about. To tell me I'd better get my act together if I wanted to come in first in the Wedding Derby. Now, do we eat the beans?'

'I'd rather talk about—oh, Harry!' She threw herself at him in total abandonment.

A half-hour later the beans were not only burned but cold. Once again he had taken her on a voyage of exploration, and pulled back at the last moment. Mickey was keyed up, unfulfilled, and frustrated, fully prepared to give the most precious gift in her possession and finding no one to give it to.

'What's the trouble?' she asked wistfully. 'Aren't I doing it right?' His fingers were busy buttoning her blouse back up. To the throat, no less.

'You're doing everything right,' he assured her. 'But too fast. Remember, little girl——'

'I'm not a little girl!'

'I can see that. Hold still, damn it. There. Reminds me of one of my father's quotes when he was telling me the facts of life. A girl uses buttons to control life. Up if she wants to warm herself, down if she wants to warm the man she's with!'

'Stop teasing, Harry. If you don't I'm going to cry all over you.' He stepped back and held up both hands in total surrender.

'Not that, lady. This is supposed to be a happy time.'

'Well, it could be happier if you weren't so—what are people in town going to say about you and me getting married? I hadn't thought about that!'

'Second thoughts, huh?'

'No, I don't have second thoughts. I'm having first thoughts. I've had second thoughts since I was fourteen. That's when I fell in love with you. Now I—Harry?'

'What?'

'Do you believe the man should be the head of the house?'

'Whoa up. What is this, a test I have to pass?'

'No, silly, just tell me. Do you?'

'Well, yes I do. Does that make you angry?'

'No,' she sighed. 'Now listen. You're the head of our house, and you say we're going to be married. Right?'

'Right.' A very cautious "right". A lawyerly "right", as if he were searching between the letters of the word for loopholes.

'So since you're the authority, and you've said, we're practically married, aren't we?'

'I——Well . . .' He stroked his chin. She reached up to do the same and was awarded a few extra prickles for her pain. His beard was growing faster than her logic could expand. 'Presuming everything you've said is correct, then what?' That lawyer again, she told herself. Him I've got to stamp out. I'll make a plan for after we're married!

He must have seen the scheming look on her face. 'No you don't, lady,' he chuckled. 'You don't trap me like that. Whatever the scheme is, I won't. Put it away.'

'*That* plan was for tomorrow,' she muttered. 'Or the week after.'

'I see. But there's something closer to that about to happen? Something you think I have to be—wait a minute. That little line of logic of yours; now I know where I've heard that. Gilbert and Sullivan, the *Mikado*! All right, woman, what are you up to?'

'I'm not up to anything,' she said in her little girl voice. 'You're the authority, and we're as good as married.' And then, more determinedly, 'So we don't have to worry about a thing, and we might as well hop into bed, mightn't we?' With an up-beat wistful ending, that sentence. Mickey was tired of waiting to see how the end of the dream turned out.

He was still chuckling, so evidently he wasn't shocked. That made her feel a tiny bit better. But not very much. She wasn't overwhelmed by his answer, and there strangely wasn't a word in the dictionary for how she felt. Perhaps there should be one? 'Whelmed'? Or even 'underwhelmed'? She tried to put both arms around him again, with about as little success as before. 'You don't agree?'

'I don't agree, little witch. I figure that we need to do something to protect your name, Mickey Devlin. I anticipate what we need is a long engagement, so that everyone, especially you and I and Papa, can get accustomed to what's coming. And I have a few things to do, you know. I intend to give up my practice in Boston, and move to Albany. I want us to live with or near Papa. He'll need a bit of company——'

'And his grandchildren,' she agreed. 'If we hurry we——'

'We're not going to hurry!'

'Yes, sir,' she said submissively.

'So now let's get some sleep,' he ordered. 'You can have the bunk and I'll take the floor.'

'No.'

'No?'

'That's right, no. If nothing is going to happen tonight, I want to go home. We have the canoe, and there's no hurry, so you can paddle as slowly as you want, and I'll be able to get something decent to eat, and sleep in my own bed.'

'Mule-headed.' He looked as if he would like to pound on the top of her head. She ducked out of the way, just in case. There's a lot I have to learn about handling men, she thought. I must spend a week remembering how Mama did it. She looked up to find him studying her quizzically.

'You don't seem to realise what a night I've had,' he complained. 'First I paddle all the way out here, then I have to fight your monstrous boyfriend, then I have to wiggle my way through the maze from "I'm not your brother" to "happily ever after". And now you want me to get out there and paddle us both back home?'

'That's exactly it,' she said firmly. 'You *do* get it right if I'm firm enough, don't you?'

Harry was still grumbling when he launched the canoe. There was a wicker chair-rest set into its stern. Essentially it was the back of a chair, but with no bottom, provided so that one could lean back against it for support. He sat there, cross-legged, and paddled. She found space in front of him and stretched out full-length, with her head in his lap. Despite all the protests the paddle stroked slowly and easily under the impulse of his hard muscles. She rolled gently with each stroke, unwilling to lose the feeling of contact, rubbing her cheekbones along the soft corduroy covering his thigh. He was not as impervious as he wanted her to believe.

The storm had fled south towards the city, leaving only shreds of high cumulus to follow. The tiny waves offered no objection to their progress. Very close by, perhaps from the mountain's shoulder, that loon laughed again, high and clear in the soft stillness of the night.

She mused as they travelled. A long engagement, he had said. Days of laughter. Nights when she might induce him to—wrong word, she told herself, giggling softly. Nights when she might seduce him to almost anything. Her mind ran riot with all the things they might do, things she had read about, things she had heard from her girlfriends. Her cheeks turned blush-red, but he could not possibly know that. Her pulse-rate jumped, but Harry was too busy with his paddle. All those nights before us, pursuing a dream. Wonder how many?

'Harry,' she asked. 'About that long engagement. Just how long did you have in mind?'

'Today's Sunday,' he reckoned. 'How about until—say—Tuesday?'

She pressed back against him, turning her head to one side to feel the tension in his thigh. 'Tuesday?' She grinned. *That* didn't leave a great deal of time for seduction! 'Harry,' she repeated, shivering deliciously, 'paddle faster!'

*Exciting, adventurous, sensual stories
of love long ago*

On Sale Now:

SATAN'S ANGEL by Kristin James

*Slater was the law in a land that was as wild and untamed
as he was himself, but all that changed when he met
Victoria Stafford. She had been raised to be a lady, but
that didn't mean she had no will of her own. Their search
for her kidnapped cousin brought them together, but they
were too much alike for the course of true love to run
smooth.*

PRIVATE TREATY by Kathleen Eagle

*When Jacob Black Hawk rescued schoolteacher
Carolina Hammond from a furious thunderstorm, he
swept her off her feet in every sense of the word, and she
knew that he was the only man who would ever make her
feel that way. But society had put barriers between them
that only the most powerful and overwhelming love could
overcome . . .*

Look for them wherever Harlequin books are sold.

Temptation™

TEMPTATION WILL BE
EVEN HARDER TO RESIST...

In September, Temptation is presenting a sophisticated new
face to the world. A fresh look that truly brings Harlequin's
most intimate romances into focus.

What's more, all-time favorite authors Barbara Delinsky, Rita
Clay Estrada, Jayne Ann Krentz and Vicki Lewis Thompson
will join forces to help us celebrate. The result? A very special
quartet of Temptations...

- **Four striking covers**
- **Four stellar authors**
- **Four sensual love stories**
- **Four variations on one spellbinding theme**

All in one great month! Give in to Temptation in September.

TDESIGN-1